TWENTY-NINE TALES FROM THE FRENCH

SELECTED AND TRANSLATED
BY
ALYS EYRE MACKLIN

WITH AN INTRODUCTORY ESSAY
ON THE FRENCH CONTE
BY
ROBERT HERRICK

Short Story Index Reprint Series

 BOOKS FOR LIBRARIES PRESS
FREEPORT, NEW YORK

First Published 1922
Reprinted 1971

INTERNATIONAL STANDARD BOOK NUMBER:
0-8369-3897-6

LIBRARY OF CONGRESS CATALOG CARD NUMBER:
72-157785

PRINTED IN THE UNITED STATES OF AMERICA

TWENTY-NINE TALES
FROM THE FRENCH

PREFACE

THE FRENCH *CONTE*

I

ALL modern literatures contain numerous examples of that shorter form of prose fiction known in English as the Short Story, although none with the possible exception of the Russian has so fully developed it into a distinct species, admirably fitted to express a racial temperament as have the French. The English experiments in this form as late as Maria Edgeworth and George Eliot were merely clumsy abbreviations of the novel, novelettes rather than true short stories, with the elaborate analyses of character, extended descriptions, and ponderous plots of the larger form. And in spite of occasional brilliant exceptions among the younger generation of English fiction writers it may be fairly said that the English temperament has never taken easily to this genre. Their technical process is too often a foreshortening of more elaborate narrative rather than a distinct and focused creation. The English mind turns more naturally to accretion and analysis than to compression and rapid synthesis.

The short story has developed more rapidly and more expertly in the United States than anywhere else outside of France and Russia, thanks perhaps to the insistent commercial demand from our innumerable magazines for entertainment with which to buoy up their heavy pages of advertising. Courses of instruction in "the art of the short story" in college and by correspondence supplement the efforts of editors and the stimulus of successful examples. Under these influences and the study of Poe and Bret Harte and O. Henry, the contemporary American short story is a much more skilful performance than its Anglo-Saxon ancestor: its practitioners have learned that the short story is something essentially different from the novelette, a form individual in structure and in purpose. But they have not yet realized in any considerable numbers that as produced in our country it is something other than the French *conte*, lacking the self-assurance, the flexibility, the universality,— the social quality in brief, which makes the French story unique among literary forms as a vehicle for the imaginative expression of the temperament and the genius of a people. The American short story, prolific and varied as it is, has a long way to go before it can adequately interpret American life and character as the French *conte* reflects the life and character of the French, in all moods and phases.

It may be said with equal justice that the French have never fully realized the possibilities of the true novel as the English and the Russians have developed this noble literary form,—that broad panorama of human affairs where a group of interrelated human beings are projected and developed organically through the passage of time. With *Les Miserables*, Balzac's magnificent improvisations, and the cosmopolitan scope of *Jean Christophe* in evidence, it is nevertheless true that the *roman, à longue haleine,* remains alien to the French genius. The prolonged exposition of a single protagonist through a multitude of episodes constitutes something less than the true novel. These differences of achievement in national literatures are deeply rooted and significant of more than literary peculiarities or of accident. The *conte* is the instinctive method of expression of a nervous, cerebral, highly civilized race, whose readers can divine from a hint the hidden implications of the artist; for whom everything does not have to be spelled out and conscientiously elaborated and illustrated. As its name implies the *conte* is a mere story, in germ the anecdote, the tale told by word of mouth with the aid of gesture and facial expression: the hearer is ever present to the imagination of the narrator. A little matter developed briefly and carefully, with a premeditated explosion, episodic and fleeting, yet casting long shadows backward and forward upon the destinies, the dramas, of the human beings involved. It is peculiarly the art of a people fond of conversation, urged to comment upon life's experience, with a power of swift analysis and comprehensive synthesis,—what we call generalization,—and above all fond of those ironic contrasts between character and circumstance which furnish the comedian with his precious substance. It is an art enjoyed by a people who have commonly a lively appreciation of the human comedy as it unrolls itself before their eyes and are willing to give it an objective attention, when imaginatively presented, quite apart from its incidence upon themselves. A social art for a social people.

2

In such a mood for such an audience all material of the human comedy, no matter how slight and evanescent it may seem, is fit for the creator's art. Much which the French story-teller deems adequate to carry his purpose seems thin and slight to the Anglo-Saxon mind. Most of the stories in the accompanying volume, examples of the contemporary *conte,* may appear to the American reader not accustomed to the French point of view unsubstantial, sometimes trivial, and doubtless would be rejected by writer and editor as too immaterial for the substance of a good short story. We expect more analysis, more plot, more incident—or what not. These appear to be but the jottings of the artist, sauntering pencil and note-book in hand down the boulevards of life,—sketches of character, notes of paradoxical situations, atmospheres, physical and spiritual, poignant facts—but not "stories"! Take for instance *The Fez,* one of the best examples in this volume of the genre. An old Turkish vagabond selling imitation jewelry to the patrons of cafés on the boulevard, content with his modest progress and situation, having forgotten his distant youth and abandoned its national dress suddenly meets the fact of the war in which his countrymen are fighting: he becomes at one stroke again the Turk, tumultuous, hidden memories and instincts rising from deep within, and he casts aside his rusty European high hat and dons his discarded fez, once more a Turk. This is nationalism, the call of race, in a single instance, with all its obscure instinctive control of human beings. Even slighter in texture is

René Bizet's *A Good Old Sort*. A dingy provincial café, a group of squalid players, a poor old
dupe, are all distinctly etched with the slightest use
of illustrative incident. It is a situation for the theater, one says, and that is often true of the French
conte:it has the distinctness, the crispness, the imme-
diacy as well as the dramatic surprise of the theater.
(In fact in descent through the *fabliaux* the modern form runs back directly to the theater.) It is
not surprising that so many French story tellers
are ambidexterous in their art, turning from story to
play and back again with the flexibility and mastery
that betrays no uncomfortable consciousness of difference in the two forms of expression. Indeed,
many *contes* are in dialogue (like Gyp's *Flirtation*
in this volume), lacking merely the material decora-
tion of the stage, and conversely it may be observed
that the French theater has found a place for the
short piece which the English and American drama
has not cultivated. A French audience, educated
daily in the *conte* of the feuilleton, is satisfied with
an evening's entertainment such as is offered at the
Grande Guignol consisting of four or five brief plays
varied in theme and manner, each one a succinct episodic treatment of life.

   If the *conte* is the most representative manner in
French fiction, through which the national instinct
for drama and observation universally expresses
itself, so the commercial vehicle of French journalism is adapted to the cultivation of this art. As
everybody knows (even the American doughboy after
a bitter and bewildered experience) the French newspaper always has been and always will be something

quite different from the English or the American product. Even the best of the French papers give seemingly so little attention to "news" or to what our journalism calls "stories," and so much more attention to the graceful treatment of life in general. Even its political leaders the French editor manages to invest with some imaginative charm—and passion, and dresses up an argument with illustration and epigram. We account for this quality in journalism by saying that the French are fond of talk. It is that and more: it is due to the fondness of the people for art, that is for the concrete and emotional realization of life. A French newspaper "story" (as of the famous "affaire") may be less filling than the corresponding American article, but it is much nearer imaginative realization, even when less authentic and less realistic. From the sprightly detailing of a scandal "in the highest circles," thinly anonymized by the use of initials, to the actual *conte* printed in the feuilleton at the bottom of the page there is but a step—and that the slightest—either in matter or method. I remember reading in one of the Paris newspapers during the early months of the war a feuilleton which consisted of a scene in dialogue between a poilu *en permission* and his wife in their apartment in the workers' quarter of Paris. The wife after two days of eager efforts to arouse her soldier man to his accustomed interest in their home and friends reproaches him for his dumbness and indifference to all about him. "Why won't you talk to us,—to me," she says to him. "Why won't you tell me about your life *làbas?*" And the poilu after reflection gravely replies,—"Those who make this war never talk about it." In that simple scene, with its exchange between the loving wife and her estranged husband, the soldier's explanation of his peculiar deadness to the civilian routine, was summed up much of the peculiar quality of the war and its effect upon the citizen soldier. Contrast this typical situation beneath the mansard in the little apartment, and its expressive dialogue, with a similar "story" in the American newspaper. The French newspaper giving voice to any and all phases of life, whether so-called actual or imagined, making no very great distinction between the two, has been the fertile forcing bed for the French story teller. The French newspapers print these *contes* by the thousands; each day they appear at the bottom of the page, as many in this volume appeared in *Le Journal*. Instead of our joke columns and special writers' columns of all sorts of odds and ends, the French have their feuilletonists—and which is the more civilized taste? Reporters turn easily from their regular work to the writing of *contes* for the feuilleton. Hence there is less difficulty for the French boy who aspires to become a writer in getting a suitable training through the newspaper than with us. The standards of accomplishment and excellence are not so far apart. And that is why apparently there are so many more competent writers of fiction in France than in England or America.

The secret of it all, I take it, is that the Frenchman does not draw that arbitrary and formal line between life and art which we serious-minded Anglo-Saxons are still inclined to set up. All the stuff of life is to the French mind good material for expres-

sion, in novel or play or story, as in newspaper report. Evidence of the effect of this way of thinking
can be found in the prolific publication during the
earlier years of the great war of diaries and books
of war experience, which while being intimate and
informal and personal had also a high imaginative
and artistic quality. I would cite Duhamel's several
war books drawn from his hospital experiences.
Each one of the episodes in *Civilization,* for instance, is something more than the report of a
"case": it is a complete *conte* done with the tender
individuality of the artist, full of perception. This
free, swift exchange between life lived and life ordered and presented imaginatively, which is charac-
teristic of French literature, has a deep cultural significance. French people express themselves commonly with the precision and the concrete visualiza-
tion of the artist. They analyze and synthesize and
select instinctively like the artist. An incident has
more than its own fleeting significance: it is illustrative of something general in human experience.
Hence comes the average excellence merely as writing of the ordinary newspaper, the boulevard play,
the war book,—yes, even the text-book! In such a
warm atmosphere of appreciation the *conte* has flour-
ished luxuriantly.

3

All the stuff of life is to the French mind good
material for expression, I have said. Just as the
trivial and the passing may be endowed with significance, so the universal and fundamental experience of
sex may not be barred from social or moral consid-

erations. The French attitude towards sex is usually misunderstood by the English and the American stranger, both in life and in literature. It is not because the French writer or his readers are more prurient or more sex-obsessed than other people that some form of sex situation appears so often in French literature. It is rather because sex being one of the universal keys to human action the Frenchman will not ignore it at the demand of a hypocritical modesty or conventional morality. He sees the sex urge specifically involved in so many human manifestations that he refuses to turn his face and pretend that it isn't so. Moreover sex is one of the few great comic themes of humanity, which the French covetously preserve. The world in these graver days has lost some of the old fields of comedy: insanity already has disappeared, and now drunkenness is passing, presently perhaps old age will no longer appeal to the civilized mind as comic. To set forth the aberrations of a deranged mind stirs our tears rather than our smiles, except among hard-minded youth. But the individual driven by sex hunger into humiliating and ridiculous perplexities still remains, at least to the French mind, a legitimate source of laughter. The human being dominated by sex retains most potently the illusion of his own personality, but to the observer his illusion is as often ridiculous as pathetic. It will be a long time before the French can be persuaded that sex should be excluded from their literature unless solemnly treated. In spite of this traditional attitude towards sex, in spite of the infinite variations in situation presented, French literature has little nastiness in it, little morbidity of sex preoccupation. For examples of that disease one must go rather to English, and—occasionally— American literature. The French attack is more often gay than somber, and if realistic at least healthy. Possibly the present volume may have been winnowed for a more puritan public than the feuilleton reaches, yet even in this collection of twenty-nine tales there are two examples of the French treatment of this common aspect of humanity,—one tragic and one gay. *When She Was Dead* sets forth the revelation over the deathbed of a woman of her dual personality in the presence of her two lovers, one who had possessed her body and the other who had held her soul. Incidentally this story is an instance of the temptation to exaggeration and the straining of circumstance in order to make evident a subtle generalization. The situation here presented may be unreal: the psychology is perfectly sound. In the farcical story of the *The Widow* and the device employed for disposing of an overstock of household furniture, the situation is also pushed to extravagance.

This I may say in passing is one of the dangers of the highly finished art of the *conte:* the temptation to the writer to lay hold of the bizarre and the excessive in order to "make his point" tellingly within the allotted compass. The conclusion of *The Last Visit* and the motivation of *The Wrist-Watch* betray this failure. The greatest masters of the *conte* have not often relied upon such *coups de théâtre.* Daudet's famous picture of the last French lesson Maupassant's marvelous *Piece of String* and *The Necklace,* as well as the Marguerittes' *Poum and the Zouave* of this volume are instances of the

sufficiency and poignancy of the simplest, most
restrained methods.

4

There is one permeating quality of the French
story as of the French character, which, alas, our own
literature is almost bereft of, and that is irony.
Irony, I take it, is in large the perception of the eternal contrast between human will and imagination and
human fate. It is the very essence of any fully civilized comprehension of life. The French abound in
this salt with which literature as life is preserved.
It is the genesis of the familiar shrug of the shoulders, the controlled and fleeting smile, the ripple of
subdued laughter that greets a subtle situation in a
French theater. We Americans do not understand
irony; we mistake it for sarcasm and are uncomfortable under it. It makes us feel that some one is
laughing at us and lowers our self-esteem. We do
not like it, if we are aware of it. And we frequently
mistakenly condemn it as the expression of a critical
instead of a "constructive" attitude in life; or in
other pollyannaish terms. Irony in its fullest reach is,
rather, the understanding of the gods, which though
bitter may be tender and kind. It is through irony
that man lifts himself momentarily above his puppet
doom and is enabled to see himself roundly, toler-
antly, and sanely. It is death to self-satisfaction and
crudity. . . .

Scarcely one of the twenty-nine stories brought together in this volume from so many different sources
but is touched somewhere with this saving quality of
irony, either in fact or in expression. The mother
leaves her son condemned to death for crime happy

in the illusion of a kiss from the woman for whom he committed his crime. The coffin intended for a dead neighbor is set down by mistake in the room of a sick woman too feeble to face the hardships of her life. The embezzler who has had the patience to serve his long prison term in the hope of ultimately enjoying his carefully hidden plunder forgets the key to its possession and drowns himself in despair. . . . Without irony the savor would fade from the French *conte*. And it is obviously the one most needed quality in our own American short story, but until that civilization which an art reflects has attained the poise which permits its appreciation it is futile to look for it. *Main Street* has not yet reached that point, which the French peasant long ago reached, where small things including himself and his affairs can be contemplated *sub specie aeternitatis,* with a gentle smile. For our Hart, Schaffner and Marx young heroes, our magazine-cover girls, our *Saturday Evening Post* millionaires would laugh themselves out of existence, at the entrance of reality.

5

These, then, are the chief characteristics of this precious French art in the multiform variety of the *conte:* a delicate and widely trained skill in presentation, a just interchange between life and art and a liberal choice of material, an ironic quality of soul capable of holding life a little way from the eyes and gently smiling at it. Other qualities of course, but these to my taste are the enduring ones. There are certain capabilities of the short fiction form which have been exploited better by others, by the Russians especially: the impression of the atmosphere of large masses of life as with Tchekof, the literal rendering of the primitive modes of the human soul as with Gorky. There may be excellencies and characteristics all our own some day to be revealed in the American magazine story. But for closeness, suppleness, breadth of treatment, for technical accomplishment and diversity, the French *conte* is as yet without real rivals.

This volume of twenty-nine stories has the quality of contemporaneousness in the sense that they are all the work of Frenchmen still living and writing. If they may be taken as adequately representative of contemporary work in this field, we must in all honesty admit that temporarily the French art of the *conte* has lost something of its rich authority from the glorious days of the great Guy. That may mean merely that no one outstanding genius is just now pouring himself into this special mold, or that the world convulsion, in this as in so many other ways a vast dissipator of energies, has scattered the *conte* material through many other channels,—books of war experience, journals and letters, and also spilled it prodigally on the bloody fields of France. Not lost irrevocably, it is reasonable to hope, but in due time to be reassembled, assimilated according to the mystic alchemy of the creative mind, renewed with all its old fecundity to give further voice to the national genius. For as long as French people live, the *conte* will fall from ironic lips and flow from skilful pens.

ROBERT HERRICK.

New York.
    November, 1921.

CONTENTS

TRISTAN BERNARD

THE LAST VISIT

By TRISTAN BERNARD

"MADAME LEON, don't bother about that petticoat now. You can finish it to-morrow. I'd rather you got on with my husband's overcoat to-day; we're going out to-night, and if the lining of the sleeve is still torn, I'll never hear the last of it. I'll give you some satinette I was keeping for a skirt . . . But tell me, Madame Léon, is there anything the matter with you? You look as if you've been crying!"

"No, Madame. There's nothing the matter."

"Come, come—something's wrong. Won't you tell me?

"I'd rather not talk about it, Madame. It's four years to-day since . . . since my poor boy . . ."

"You have lost a son?"

"Alas, Madame! It was the way I lost him that . . ."

"I won't ask you . . ."

"You'll have heard them talking of Hucheux? . . . That's my real name, Madame. Here in Paris it doesn't matter much . . . it all happened away in the country at home. I ought to tell you that when I was twenty I was married to a young man who was nineteen."

"You took a great fancy to each other?"

"No, Madame. We were cousins. We just thought of it one day because we knew each other so well. We were fond of each other like cousins. We never thought of anything else. He was big and kind, and he was very retiring with nothing to say for himself. We were only married six weeks. He got a chill and died. I was in the family way, and the baby was born eight months afterwards.

"He got the chill at his aunt's funeral, who used to have a little draper's shop in the town we lived in. I took the shop over for the sake of having something behind me, being alone in the world, and it was better than going out sewing by the day. And I brought the little one up all alone, not wanting to marry any one else in spite of there being others after me; there were three of them telling me I was pretty and asking me to marry them; yes, three, and one of them was a paymaster's sergeant who made over forty francs a month doing the bills for a butcher.

"My little one grew up nicely. I sent him to school. He was one of the best boys in the school, and a scholar, too, always first, Madame, for arithmetic and writing. Till he was eighteen, no one could have found a fault with that lad of mine. Never wanting to go out, always reading. I thought that was good for him, and all the time it was turning his brain. I thought he would be like his father with women, a man who knew no more about such things than I did. And then, Madame, all of a sudden, in the house of a school friend, he got to know a lady who was the wife of a man who had a shop near mine.

"One day he came to me and said:

" 'Mother, I want four thousand francs. I must have it!'

"He knew I'd been able to put a little money by. Of course I asked him what he wanted it for. At first he wouldn't say, and then there he was telling me a long story, that he'd got intimate with this lady, that the husband of the lady was going to fail in business, and that he wanted to stop his failing. Of course I said I wouldn't give him the money. He got into an awful state, and made a scene. But what could I do? I couldn't give him all that money. It was for him I was saving it. And then I didn't know what he'd be wanting next, where it would all stop. And nobody gives away money like that.

" 'All right,' he says to me. 'If that's how it is, I'll go and ask my god-father for it.'

"His god-father lived out of town, in the last house of the suburb. He'd been a cooper, and was getting on for eighty.

" 'I know your god-father,' says I. 'He won't lend you anything, my poor lad. You'll only turn him against you, and it'll be a pity to do that.'

"Well, he didn't listen to me, just went all the same. That was a little after supper. I sat up for him till eleven. Then I went to bed.

"I felt a bit anxious, but he'd slept out once or twice before . . . The next morning there was still no sign of him. It was market day, and I went with my basket to the square. And, Madame, this is what I heard. There were two old women selling vegetables, and one of them says: 'Yes,' she says to the other, 'he didn't offer no resistance. An old man like that of over a hundred. He hit him on the head with a brass candlestick! It'll likely have been some tramp thinking there was sure to be money in the old cooper's house.'

"At that moment, Madame, how I managed to stand straight I don't know. My legs were trembling under me. I didn't know where I was. I could hear the hens clucking and the people talking, and the noise went on without stopping. Then I heard other people saying things about it, and they were making it out different—that it was a soldier on leave who had done it, and they'd got him, and he was in prison . . . Then I felt happy. I'd never been so happy in my life . . . The noise of the market sounded pleasant. There was a nice smell of butter and of the feathers of the fowls.

"I'd forgotten what I'd come to buy, whether it was a cabbage or some carrots. And then they were at it again, talking about the same thing. And this is what I heard.

"A young lady who was the chemist's servant was saying she didn't know who had committed the crime. I went up to her and I said:

" 'It was a soldier on leave that did it.'

" 'No, you're wrong!' says the girl. 'They arrested a soldier, but they let him go at once. He told them right enough where he was when it happened.'

"I went home without buying anything. I couldn't think of anything. I felt sick, and my legs were shaking. And then, Madame, when I went into my son's room, what do you think I saw? Henri, with a pail of water on the floor, and washing his coat in it.

"Then I began to cry and call out like as if I had gone mad. He cried, too, and he told me to be quiet.

" 'What have you done, oh, what have you done, my Henri?'

"And I cried and cried, just like I'm crying now."

"And weren't you a little frightened of him? Didn't you keep away from him?"

"From my little one, Madame? . . . Oh, how terrible it was to see him like that! . . . He sat there, stock-still, never thinking of getting away from the police. It was me that had to tell him to go. But he couldn't go by the station. He could ride a bicycle well, but he had sold his to give the money to this woman, so I gave him the price of another, and enough to keep him for a little while. He kissed me and left me alone, and I had to hide his clothes by myself. They weren't stained, but they were wet, and the police might have asked why he had washed cloth things that ought to be sent to be cleaned. When it was dark I buried them in the garden.

"I didn't see any one till next day, and then two men from the police-station came to ask where my son was. And the Inspector came himself. He looked everywhere without finding anything. I told them my son had been away from home for several days. If only you could have seen how quiet I was. I didn't know myself, for I was always timid talking to people, and there I was lying to these gentlemen as if I was speaking the truth. But I had to, and I did it.

"There wasn't much evidence against Henri, and they didn't know where he was. He could have got right away and kept hidden, but—can you believe it? He came back in two days' time. He couldn't keep away from this woman. He had always been such a good lad, quiet-like and timid, but since she'd got hold of him, he wasn't afraid of anything. He'd come back to see her pass by in the street. He hung about her house in the rue des Chaumières. A little boy saw him, and told another who knew he was wanted, and they went to Chevalet, the Inspector. And Chevalet and another man had nothing to do but walk up to him, and take him like you take a little bird in your hand.

"Everybody was very kind to me. They didn't spare themselves in doing things for me. It seemed to please them to be generous to me, and they kept on trying to comfort me by saying it was not my fault if I had brought such a creature into the world. They said he was a hardened criminal, a terrible monster, because the head of his god-father had been battered in by a candlestick. I knew it had happened when he was out of his mind, and that he had hit like a brute because he didn't know what he was doing. I said it often to his lawyer, but he never told them. He never listened to what I said. I'd done wrong in going to that lawyer! He was a young man who was always busy with other things, getting up meetings for young lawyers, and he didn't have many people go to him. He was big and dark, and was always stroking his long, curly beard. I was very angry at the trial. I could see quite well that all he was thinking of was showing himself off with his 'Monsieur le Président' here, and his 'Monsieur l'Avocat-Général' there. Me and my boy and his trouble, it was all the same to him!

"The worst time was when the jury went out, and we were waiting in the court. The usher, who looked after the jury, came in before they did. He'd been taking the lamps in to them . . . He said something to the lawyers. And they looked at me.

"When they brought Henri in to hear the sentence, he stood up straight and listened. Then he looked about, as if he was trying to find where I was. But he didn't see me. Then he turned to the policeman. He touched his hat as he passed him. And he went out as if nothing had happened.

"I hadn't said anything to the lawyer about Fanny, the woman, because Henri had made me swear not to talk about her. You'll understand I didn't like her, because it was her that had made all our trouble. And then she'd never done a thing since my lad was in prison. She'd never even said a word to any one about it. I suppose she was thinking of her husband and her children . . . When Henri spoke to me about her, and seemed so sad not to see her, I wanted to tell him he mustn't blame her. But I never could. I felt queer about it, as if I was jealous because he thought more of her than of me. I knew that children were like that, but it hurt me.

"The lawyer had gone to Paris to try and get him off. Every one said it was fine of him to put himself out to go and see the President of the Republic. But I knew he did it because it pleased him to make himself talked of, and to see the Président . . . And it wasn't any good."

"It must have been a dreadful time for you!"

"I'm afraid to think of it, Madame. But somehow sometimes I didn't suffer at all, I didn't think of anything at all. People used to come and see me at nights. They used to talk about the trial and one thing and another. I used to make hot wine for them. It used to seem as if I was dreaming it all, as if nothing had happened.

"Then one night, all of a sudden, I felt it was coming soon, and I lay and trembled all over. And I saw I must always try and find out overnight which morning it was going to be, so I shouldn't have such an awful night again, being afraid of what I should hear when I got up. And every evening when it grew dark and the train from Paris was coming in, I used to wait near where the passengers come out. That was how I saw the man with his two assistants. They had on gray overcoats and soft hats; they had big packages wrapped in canvas, and they saw them put safely on a lorry.

"It was about seven o'clock at night. I had seen Henri the morning before, and I was to go and see him again in two days. I could not part with my little one like that without saying good-by.

"I knew I wouldn't be allowed in the prison out of hours. But I had talked to Monsieur Bellot, the chief warder, and I thought he might let me in. It's queer how you remember things, but I can always see the dish of potatoes on the table in his sitting-room. He was eating with his lady and children. I went in and I began to cry and couldn't speak. He knew all about next morning, and he didn't ask me what I was crying for.

" 'Monsieur Bellot,' I says to him, 'I must see him once again!'

" 'Ah, Madame,' he says, 'that I can't do. I'd lose my place here if I did.'

"But when he saw how miserable I was, he had

pity on me, and he said I could go with him on his rounds and just kiss my boy as I passed . . . So we went together down the corridors. It was a very old prison, and it was all very dark. You could hardly see the lamps at the end of the corridors. Monsieur Bellot had got a lantern, but the light only shone on the ground.

"We went up to the second floor, and we stopped before a door.

" 'It's here,' says he. 'Kiss him through the bars.'

" 'Hucheux!' he says quietly. 'Here's some one come to say good-by to you!'

"I couldn't see him through the bars, but I could feel he was there, and I heard him say softly:

" 'Is it you, Fanny?'

"And he leant his face against mine, and kissed me like no one had ever kissed me in my life . . ."

"Poor, poor thing! You must have felt broken-hearted at his thinking of the other . . ."

"Me, Madame? I never thought of anything like that. He was so happy! so happy! I could feel it in the way he kissed me. I was only afraid of one thing, and that was that he'd find out it wasn't her. And I was glad that the warder dragged me away. And that last night that I'd been terrified to think of, that I'd never thought that I could live through— well, I just fell asleep, and didn't wake till late in the morning. At first when I came to, I felt I could never get up again, knowing it was all over. Then I thought of how he had died happy, and all day long I sat and knitted and knitted, not saying anything to any one, at a jersey with big stitches that I had just begun, and I got it finished in the day."

ANDRÉ BIRABEAU

II

THE BARBER'S MIRACLE

By ANDRE BIRABEAU

"I THINK I'll call at the barber's as I come home," said Monsieur Berledin.

Madame Berledin shrugs her shoulders.

"But your hair is not so very long! And if you think it will add to your beauty . . . When a man earns as little as you do, he has no business to waste money, he should try to save every farthing. Still . . ."

The "still" means consent. M. Berledin loses no time in shutting the door behind him, and once safely outside, smiles happily. It is not that he finds any pleasure in putting himself in the hands of the barber. His "beauty"—good heavens, he has very little illusion about himself! Look at him: is there anything of the dandy about the lock of hair that projects stiffly from beneath his hat, the beard that is neither round, nor square, nor oval, whose hairs grow in a tangled mass like rank grass in an abandoned garden, the mustache that droops into his mouth, yellowed by tobacco, a trap to catch drops of wine and soup, an adornment that makes M. Berledin look like a kindly, rough-haired terrier? He would willingly give up the services of clippers and scissors for months at a time; in fact, he finds that a mass of thick, long hair is very useful in affording a good grip for his hand when he is pursuing some fugitive idea.

But M. Berledin has his little stratagems. It is impossible to know how long you may be kept at the barber's; one hour, an hour and a half, two hours even . . . What can Madame Berledin answer when she is told in an innocent tone, "There were ten others before me," or "My dear, the assistant was short-sighted, and cut my hairs one by one." Madame Berledin has not the slightest suspicion that her husband enters the shop like a hurricane with a "Quick! It doesn't matter how it's done, but be quick!" that as soon as it is over, brushing aside the hand-mirror presented by the capillary expert, and disdaining the small boy with the clothes-brush, he looks at his watch and reflects, "I have at least thirty-five minutes!" and off he goes, almost at a run, to the quays, diving with delight into the dusty boxes of the second-hand booksellers. Happy minutes—and always more than thirty-five, for M. Berledin grants himself various extensions of time. Couldn't there have been still one more client before him at the barber's?

In the atmosphere of these dirty, discolored books, M. Berledin becomes another person. Life seems well worth living, inspired as he is by the hope, ever fervent though never realized, of making some wonderful discovery during his search among the volumes . . . While he handles the books he feels as if he owns them. He reads a word here, a sentence there, touches on a hundred different subjects, and no idler strolling along the boulevard to look at the pretty women who pass by is as happy as he.

But these blissful half-hours are seldom enjoyed by M. Berledin. Madame Berledin is a very difficult person. Severe and disagreeable, she talks loudly, gives harsh orders, and nags incessantly. He is never allowed a minute for quiet meditation. She has completely forgotten how delighted she was, lacking beauty, youth and fortune, to come across a man who would marry her; she now believes she could have made a much better match, and blames her husband for having proposed to her. She taunts him with his modest tastes, his unselfish gentleness, and the small sum he earns by writing dry articles for philosophic magazines. Seeing, however, that he is unfitted for any other work, she keeps him at it, morning, noon and night, with his study door half-open so that she may see that he does not sit yawning or waste time in smoking cigarettes.

Mr. Berledin bows his back to his burden, for he cannot stand quarrels and scenes, but he dissembles, and the visit to the barber's is one of his stratagems.

To-day he will certainly have three-quarters of an hour to himself; an empty chair stands waiting for him.

"A hair-cut, and trim my beard. As quickly as possible!"

He puts on the wrapper himself to save time. Alas! the assistant seems to be of the chattering sort. He is a tall, thin young man, clean-shaven, with feverish eyes, who gesticulates freely and makes remarks to himself as well as to the client. M. Berledin decides to rout him by a masterly silence.

"Hair-cut and trim the beard? . . . Very good, sir. Quite short, I suppose? The clippers? No?

You are wrong. It's very bad to wear the hair long.
This hot weather, too, and it is frightfully close to-
day . . . It is extremely bad to have such a lot of
hair on the head. It weighs you down. I couldn't
stand it; when I found how hot it was this morning,
I took all mine off. I had curly hair and a mustache, and off they came. Clean. Yes, sir, clean off!
Let me try the clippers. You won't? You're making
a mistake. When it's so hot, so very hot . . . Your
head a bit to the right, please. Besides, men oughtn't
to be allowed to have long hair. Yes, sir, long hair
ought to be forbidden. All vices have their origin
in the hair. The clippers, sir, the clippers—that's the
remedy. For everything. What was Samson? A
bully and a brute. Delilah comes along. She uses
the clippers, and immediately Samson becomes inoffensive . . . What do they do to reclaim convicts?
They clip them . . . To make soldiers brave and
disciplined? Clip them . . . The clippers! the clippers! The head to the left, if you please. A beard
is a mask, and so is a mustache. People don't see
you as you are if you wear a beard and mustache;
you deceive them. Clean-shave a man, and he will
appear as he really is. Clippers! Clippers! Napoleon, what was he? Clean-shaven. It is the only way
to settle social problems. You watch and see how
few love-crimes there will be when I have passed my
clippers over the head of every woman in Paris. I
went to explain this to Poincaré. He wouldn't listen
to me. He's got a beard. All politicians have
beards. But I mean to run my clippers through every
beard. If life is full of misery, it is because God has
a beard. But I'll run my clippers through His beard,

too! All, all of them—the bristly pigs! I'll clip them! I'll clip them! I'm the great clipper . . . Ah! Ah! . . . Ah! . . ."

They succeed in rescuing M. Berledin from these formidable hands. It is a much more difficult task to master the Great Clipper; he has jumped up on the marble basin where he brandishes his clippers and scissors in a most disconcerting manner. At last he slips on a piece of soap and falls, and they take him away. The saloon is in a ferment of emotion. The assistants argue.

"Who could have suspected it? Of course he has seemed a bit strange these last few days . . . It must be the heat . . . It's lucky for you, sir,"— they turned to M. Berledin—"that he didn't happen to have a razor in his hand!"

Probably it was very lucky for M. Berledin, but that does not make his condition less deplorable. Shrinking with fear, he had not been able to stave off the assault, and three drives with the clippers are quickly inflicted. The Great Clipper had plied his instrument haphazard and with great force; the first stroke had done nothing but cut a great gash in the hair above the right temple, but the second, starting at the left ear, had reached the middle of the head, and the third had traced an irreparable ravine right through one side of the beard. The assistants who gather around the poor man have difficulty in hiding their amusement. The proprietor alone is anxious; he apologizes profusely and murmurs reassuring words:

"The damage is not beyond repair, sir . . . there's no doubt, I'm afraid, that the head must be close-cropped, but we can still make something of the beard. . . . What do you think, Alcide?"

Alcide is the most experienced artist in the establishment. He does not reply at once. He shakes his head doubtfully. It will be a delicate piece of work. But Alcide has talent, and is proud of his skill. Finally he says:

"I can certainly leave a tuft below the lip . . . even an Imperial . . . Perhaps I might manage a Royal. But I only say 'perhaps.' We shall see."

Alcide is too modest. He succeeds admirably, and here is M. Berledin adorned with an Imperial as trim as if he had always worn it. M. Berledin stares in the glass with amazement. He does not recognize himself. It is thirty years since he saw his cheeks, and they surprise him. They are two round cheeks, young, unwrinkled, and tinged with rose.

"It's odd," says M. Berledin. "It's very odd."

He would have liked to go on looking at himself for a long time. He is full of conflicting feelings: astonishment, sadness, and also some pleasure. . . . This is how he used to look at twenty, when, full of ardor, self-confident, and audacious, he used to hold forth in the student's club and write violent attacks on members of the Académie for the minor press.

And he can also see in this face the features of his dashing brother, the Captain in the Merchant Service. M. Berledin keeps on staring at himself.

"Me—can it possibly be me?"

When he gets up to leave the shop the proprietor is still making excuses. Preoccupied, Mr. Berledin murmurs:

"It doesn't matter . . . it doesn't matter at all
. . ."

He is not sincere. He knows perfectly well that
it does matter. The proof lies in the fact that instead of going down the boulevard towards the quays
where the dusty books are waiting for him in their
boxes, he turns the other way. What will Madame
Berledin say? There will be a scene, of course. The
injustice of it! As if he could have guessed when
he took that seat in the barber's that he was placing
himself in the hands of a lunatic. And those unjust
scenes are the worst of all; she is always more violent when she is in the wrong.

M. Berledin literally dare not go home. The
quiet garden of the Luxembourg is there before him,
a delightful refuge for the idle. M. Berledin takes
his uneasiness and fears to the cool paths where the
shade from the big trees spreads out like water. He
sits down on a bench where two youths are talking
with great animation. They are discussing military
matters with more heat than knowledge; one of them,
thwarted and at the end of his arguments, turns suddenly towards M. Berledin saying:

"Sir, will you give your opinion? One sees at once
that you have been an officer . . . your face, your
bearing, everything about you . . . Am I right in contending that the system of fortifications . . ."

M. Berledin confesses with some confusion that
he is merely a philosopher. With some confusion,
but also with much inward satisfaction. Does he
really give this impression of robust military self-
confidence? To be sure, he is not fifty yet, but . . .

Involuntarily he throws back his shoulders, holds

up his head, handles his stick more smartly, and walks along the path with firmer tread. A young woman crosses his path and smiles at him. And a very charming smile, too. No doubt it is that young woman's business to smile at people like that, but would she even have looked at the M. Berledin of an hour ago with his fuzzy beard, drooping mustache and air of philosophic resignation? . . . The new M. Berledin no longer thinks of leaving the cool garden with its shady paths, fountains and statues, and it is no longer only fear that keeps him there; it is also the thought of the deadly weariness of seeing Madame Berledin . . .

Thirty years ago he walked these same paths full of ambition. The most august institution inspired no fear in him in those days, nor in those days could a young woman have smiled at him with impunity. M. Berledin suddenly becomes aware that for twenty-five years he has never thought of any woman but his wife, and it makes him wonder—and feel sad. He admits that he has never even dared to wish to do so; he has been too afraid of his wife. Not at first, for he was in love with her, but as she grew more and more dominating, he had grown more humble, and she had soon become a tyrant.

M. Berledin discovers that for twenty-five years he has been a poor worm. And he thinks of his brother, the sea-captain, who has a sweetheart in every port, sweethearts who adore him, and who will stand anything from him; his brother, the sea-captain, whom he now resembles with his Imperial . . .

Dusk is falling when at last he goes home. A

woman, so taken aback that she forgets to be furious, is waiting for him . . .

"Good heavens! Who are you? How did you
get the latch-key? What—*you!* What have you
been doing to yourself? . . . You look absurd—
ridiculous! And coming in late like this! Where
have you been?"

Quite naturally, and without any premeditation,
M. Berledin makes an amazing reply:

"Be quiet! If I choose to have my beard trimmed
—and if I choose to come in late—I suppose I am
master in my own house?"

The words suit his looks so exactly that Madame
Berledin stands thunder-struck. And without a word,
she lowers her eyes and bows her head.

RENÉ BIZET

III

A GOOD OLD SORT

By René Bizet

IT was a soaking rain. It soaked the sky, the roofs, the walls; it soaked even the ceiling of a certain café, sole refuge of the tourist stranded at Beltesse-sur-Isle for his sins, and the bugbear of commercial travelers.

Despite his sixty-five years, M. Alfred Lardin made its melancholy acquaintance. Sent to the town by Ducoin, Dubois & Cie. (a house well known in the business world of Paris, but without interest for the Beltessians) to get orders for boot-laces, he had in vain bombarded all the shops with samples. He had been given the order of the boot in another sense, as if they were afraid that he concealed, under the innocent guise of his useful wares, some dangerous and deadly explosive.

Crestfallen, he had drifted into the café, that harbor where the commercial traveler, like an old ship, puts in to refit his tackling. He watched through the windows the rain falling in floods, and ever and anon his eyes wandered to the landlady who sat in a state of hard-breathing somnolence. The spirit of dullness coiled about all the upholstery, like a famished and too affectionate cat.

To rouse himself, M. Alfred gave a call. The

landlady woke with a start; the dusty and witch-like head of a servant-girl was thrust through a doorway.

"A pack of cards!" he ordered.

This was brought him, and the gas was turned up. And under the sickly lights of the fluttering jets, M. Alfred made combinations which would not combine, as always happens in such cases, and as only too frequently happened in his.

All of a sudden, carriage-wheels were heard outside; then they stopped. The door opened. Six persons entered, three men and three women, the former with faces clean-shaven, blue with cold, lined with minute wrinkles, and not too prepossessing; the latter with golden hair straggling over highly-rouged features, which, without that embellishment, would have claimed the respect due to advanced years. Their entry caused a sort of panic. The servant came on the scene with excited exclamations, and spinning about all ways at once. "Here, stop all this rushing round," called out one of the arrivals in a deep voice, "and bring us some steaming hot grog!"

M. Alfred threw down his cards, took stock of himself in a glass where the flies had left abundant traces of their social gatherings, and by way of making his presence known, coughed politely. Thereupon, as if by common impulse, the six persons turned, gave him nods of acknowledgment, and sat down by his side. The servant continued her frantic revolutions. The landlady had vanished into some unknown underground region.

"What a comforter it is!" exclaimed one of the

golden-haired ladies, apparently referring to the grog.

"What weather it is!" sighed another.

"Fat lot of receipts we are likely to take!" whimpered a tearful-looking gentleman.

Though he had not a discerning eye, M. Alfred thought he might be justified in the opinion that he had the honor of hobnobbing with comedians, and derived therefrom so much pride that he ventured to introduce himself.

"M. Alfred Lardin, commercial traveler, at your service."

"Delighted, Monsieur!" said he who seemed to be the manager of the company. "Mlles. Eliane, Lebon, Josette; MM. Tambois, Galon, and your humble servant, Charles Pantu, artistes of the principal theaters of Foligny, and here to play this evening in our masterpiece, 'So Much the Worse If Your Sister Is Ill.' "

"Very much honored, I'm sure," declared M. Alfred.

And then they lit cigarettes. They discoursed of plays, of artistes; M. Tambois gave an imitation of Sarah Bernhardt; M. Galon recalled his successes; the atmosphere of the café became animated and blue with acrid smoke. It was good to be there, snug and warm, while outside the sluices of a sky gone mad seemed to be opening.

Suddenly, in one of those pauses which are said to signify the passage of angels, a tragic note was struck. "I have lost my part!" screamed Mlle. Eliane. Five agitated voices were raised in response

to this heartfelt cry. M. Alfred thought himself
in duty bound to join in the distressful chorus.

"Where have you lost it?" asked M. Tambois.

"How do I know? At the station or on the way
to the hotel when I opened my bag."

Instinctively every one turned towards the street.
They could hardly distinguish anything now, but they
heard the beating of the indefatigable rain on the
panes, as on a drum, as if it were keeping time to a
funeral march.

"Well, rain or no rain, I must go and look for it,"
said Mlle. Eliane.

Her companions gazed at one another, hesitating
between duty and personal comfort. But M. Alfred
left them no time to display their gallantry. He
raised his hand deprecatingly: "I won't permit it,
Mademoiselle . . . I, myself . . ." one of the gentlemen interposed. Mlle. Eliane made up her lips
into the form of a grateful smile. The obliging old
man took his umbrella, overcoat and hat, and went
out under the pelting rain, as in the old days of
siege-warfare they went out under a rain of grape-
shot.

"Good old sort, that!" said M. Galon.

*   *   *   *   *   *   *

M. Alfred commenced his search. From the café
he went up to the station, and from the station down
again to the café—a good three miles altogether.
He had almost to swim for it. He rummaged about
in gutters swollen into torrents, splashed through
puddles, floundered in young quagmires, plunged into

treacherous holes full of mud, absorbed and dripped water like a super-saturated sponge, crouched down over miry accumulations, and for two hours, like some heroic diver in submarine depths, pursued his exhaustive inquisition. All in vain; he could not find the manuscript. He fished out and carried back three dirty scraps of paper which might perhaps . . .

At last he opened the café door. He presented himself, a horrible object, daubed with slime and mud, and looking like a cold-meat pie, ashamed of his failure, yet proud of the sacrifice he had made, the extent of which was written large on his overcoat in great patches of clinging mud.

"Ah!" shuddered the company.

"Sorry," exclaimed Eliane briskly. "I have found my part . . . It was in the pocket of my water-proof."

M. Alfred sustained the blow without wincing. "Have you?" he murmured. "Well, well . . . so much the better," and came forward to take the seat he had occupied.

M. Tambois, his nearest neighbor, shrank from him visibly. M. Alfred did not notice it. He took it a little to heart, however, that they made no further allusion to his wanderings. Mlle. Eliane might at least have given him a smile. But the conversation of the company slipped away from the subject altogether, and soared into the regions of high art, and hotels with fixed tariffs.

M. Tambois suddenly sniffed with unnecessary emphasis. "I say . . ." he exclaimed . . . "there's a smell as if some old poodle was in the room!"

Every one sniffed with emphasis. It was true; a smell of moist dog had crept insidiously through the apartment, and was contending successfully with the cheap scents with which the feminine charms of the company were intermingled.

The ineffable M. Alfred intervened promptly: "Don't disturb yourselves; I'll look under the seats . . . perhaps it is the house-dog." And before any one could move, he was on his knees under the table looking for the offending animal.

Such a display of innocence exasperated M. Pantu.

"Why, it's you . . . you yourself that smell like that . . . like a tank of stale salt beef . . . ugh! the idea of coming in here in that filthy state at the risk of upsetting these ladies who, perhaps, thanks to you, won't be able to get through their parts to-night . . ."

From beneath the table M. Alfred raised a face dignified by resignation, "Me? You really think it's me?"

"I haven't a doubt of it," said Mlle. Eliane.

The old man got on his feet with a heartbroken look and trembling lips, a ridiculous but touching figure with the air of a very poor man who is ashamed of his poverty. And quietly, without demonstration, strewing low-voiced apologies like bunches of withered violets, he went out. The rain was still falling persistently, falling as if it would never stop.

"Good old sort, that!" said M. Galon once more.

"I thought he wasn't going to take the hint," remarked M. Tambois.

"You see, my dears, that's just how it is," explained M. Pantu to the ladies, shrugging his shoulders. "It's this sort of thing that disgusts me with being on tour. . . . One has to mix with all kinds of inferior people . . ."

FRÉDÉRIC BOUTET

IV

FORCE OF CIRCUMSTANCES

By Frédéric Boutet

ONE afternoon when the boulevards were crowded, the Portly Gentleman suddenly felt something strange moving in the pocket of his overcoat,
and made a quick grab at it. He seized a small,
icy-cold hand, and gripped it with all his strength,
which was considerable. At the same moment he
heard a moan of pain, and caught sight of the thief;
it was a little boy in rags, so thin that the bones
seemed to be coming through his skin, and green
with a fear that prevented him from moving or
speaking.

The first impulse that moved the Portly Gentleman was indignant anger:

"You little thief! You young blackguard! At
your age! Putting your hand into other people's
pockets! Just wait till I get a policeman!"

The youngster did wait, livid, distraught with
fear. Shaken like a plum-tree by the Portly Gentleman, he seemed likely to fall in pieces, but he remained silent and resigned. A crowd gathered, and
gave vent to the various platitudes by which people
like to explain what everybody understands.

The Portly Gentleman, dragging or rather carrying the child with him, took several furious steps.

But he was naturally a good-hearted man, and he had a vague idea of the meaning of philanthropy. He suddenly became conscious of the extraordinary contrast they presented; he, enormous in his rich fur coat; the thief, so tiny in his tatters. He felt confusedly the strange inferiority of being the complainant in such circumstances. Besides, the crowd annoyed him.

"Wait a bit, I'll take you there in a cab, to the police-station," he said.

He called a taxi, and pushing the still unresisting child into it, set him down on the front seat, still keeping a grip on him.

"Now then, tell me the truth," he ordered in a terrible voice. "What's your name? How old are you? What do your parents do? How long have you been a pickpocket?"

But the thief broke into such convulsive sobs that the Portly Gentleman was afraid he would be suffocated, and alarmed, he tried to soothe him:

"Don't cry; answer!"

A shrill, small voice filtered through the sobs.

"I'm nine." (He looked six.) "Me father died two years ago. Me mother's ill and can't work. We've got nothin' to eat, and no fire, and the kids are all crying . . ."

"The kids?" asked the Portly Gentleman in surprise.

"Yes, me little sisters; there's three of 'em; there's two of 'em dead. I'm called Victor."

The Portly Gentleman loosed his hold on the cold little hands; he looked into the wan little face where the tears were washing furrows in the dirt. He snuffled:

"Where does she live, your mother?" he asked.

The child gave an address in a distant quarter in the neighborhood of Gentilly. The gentleman put his head out of the window and gave an order to the driver. The driver, on his box, gave a start of dismay.

"You'll at least give me the return-fare, sir," he complained, disgusted.

"Naturally," said the Portly Gentleman.

And they ran past the police-station without stopping.

The child was a little calmer, and his companion continued his questions:

"Tell me, how long have you been thieving, and who taught you?"

"This is the first time; I never did it before. Ugène showed me how."

"Who is Ugène?"

"I dun'no. He spoke to me in the street. He's about as old as me. But he knows his way about; he's clever. He showed me for a joke . . . on a drunk man . . . but I didn't take anything from the drunk man. And to-day I tried. We'd nothin' but three potatoes all day yesterday. And the kids was all crying. . . . And they're turning us out of our room. And this morning I was going to sell some vi'lets that a woman that lives beside us gave me, and a p'liceman took me to the station because I hadn't a license, and they took the vi'lets away . . . And I've got to give ninepence to the woman, and I'll get a hiding if I don't pay . . . And then I begged, and no one gave me nothing . . . Then I tried . . . I tried on you . . . I'm down on my luck . . . You won't have me put in quod, sir, will you? I won't do it again, I promise I'll never try it again! I don't know what me mother would say if she knew . . . You won't, sir, you won't put me into quod? . . ."

"I'm going with you to your home to see if you've been telling me the truth," said the Portly Gentleman pompously. "I will then decide what I am going to do."

Silence fell between them . . . Though he was still gulping down his sobs, the child began to take a timid pleasure in being in an automobile. The Portly Gentleman tried to meditate on the inequalities of the human lot. The taxi was now running through a district unknown to this fortunate gentleman who lived in a fashionable part of Paris, and considered that civilization ended at the Observatoire. They passed through curious streets, some of them dangerous, and finally they stopped before a tumble-down and leprous building.

"You'd better be as quick as you can, sir. This is the sort of place where people get murdered," said the chauffeur between his teeth, as he looked at the ragged aborigines who crowded to their doors to see the taxi.

But they were only the inquisitive poor, and the Portly Gentleman had resolved to carry it through. Guided by his thief, he stumbled up three flights of broken and evil-smelling stairs, and went into a room the like of which he had not yet seen, for it consisted of the ceiling, the walls, and a tiled floor on which were two mattresses, two broken chairs, a broken table, and a broken and empty stove. A wretched woman sat at a gaping window sewing at some rags, among which the Portly Gentleman saw a waxen-faced infant that looked as if it were dead. A little girl of eight was sorting some dirty feathers in a corner and another, still smaller, lay shivering on one of the mattresses. It was terribly cold and growing dark.

The Portly Gentleman gazed at all this with horror. It was the first time he had seen a poverty-stricken home, and it greatly impressed him. A sort of sudden shame took possession of him; it seemed to him as if he were some odious oppressor, and more ridiculous than he felt a little while ago on the boulevard. He had prepared some magnanimous and highly-moral remarks, but he could not remember a word of them. But he was obliged to say something, for the woman was looking at him in stupefied amazement. Making a violent effort, he managed to blurt out in a bleating sort of voice:

"It's all right . . . there's nothing wrong . . . the child will explain . . . it's nothing . . . a mistake . . . allow me . . ."

A coin glittered on the table. The Portly Gentleman was already floundering down the staircase. Thoroughly upset, he gave a sigh of relief when he found himself once more in the taxi that took him back to his own world.

*   *   *   *   *   *   *

Meanwhile, in the garret, the bewildered mother was trying to get some explanation out of Victor, who was disinclined to give any. When at length she got at the truth, she burst into despairing tears.

"It was all we had; my God, it was all that was left, being honest," she sobbed. "Your poor father would sooner have died of hunger than touch a ha'penny that wasn't his. . . . My God, my God, what a thing! . . . Victor, my little Victor, a thief! . . . You, a thief! What's happened to you? Have you gone mad? My God, it's not possible!"

But Victor, who had cried so bitterly in the taxi, had suddenly become impassive.

"It was Ugène that showed me," he explained coldly, "and if the gentleman didn't say anything . . . he's given us twenty francs, and he gave me a ride in a taxi."

"But if he'd called a policeman, you wicked boy, you'd ha' been in prison."

"Oh, no. Ugène knows how to work it. The gentlemen never put you in quod. It's Ugène's father who told him. When you see a big one who looks rich, you just put your hand in his pocket and he catches you, and you tell him you've had nothing to eat for three days . . . then they come to your house, and give you money. You needn't be afraid of them; you never get worse than a smack on the head; when you're little, they don't send you to quod. Ugène's been doing it four months, and he sometimes gets forty francs in a week. His father stops in bed all day, like as if he was ill and out of work. And when Ugène comes back with the gentleman, his father pretends he wants to get up and give Ugène a hiding, and he tells the gentleman he's honest and—and like that. And the gentleman stops

him hiding Ugène, and gives him something . . .
sometimes five francs, sometimes more, never less.
. . . And we haven't got anything, and the gentleman can see it's all right here . . . I got to do something 'cos I'm too little to work."

"But not that! Never! I won't have you doing
that . . . Swear that you'll never do it again, never,
never . . ."

Victor made no reply. With the twenty francs
there was a fire in the stove, soup, corned beef, and
they were able to pay something on account to the
landlord. But by the end of the week the last halfpenny had gone. One day there were not even three
potatoes between them, and Victor went out to gather
vegetable peelings from the dustbins to make soup.

Next day he looked his mother resolutely in the
face, and said:

"I'm going out."

She cried out: "Victor!" and tried to hold him
back, but he escaped and vanished. She went back
to the room.

"Oh! look, mother," cried the eldest of the little
girls an hour later, "the woman next door's given
me these bits o' coal . . . shall I make a fire? We
won't be so cold."

The poor woman seemed to hesitate.

"No," she said at last, her face flushing. "It's
better not to have a fire . . . Suppose your brother
meets some one again like he did the other day . . ."

And with resignation, the pallid infant on her
knees, she sat down and began to stitch at some rags,
preparing the scene.

MAX AND ALEX FISCHER

V

ARMY TIME

By MAX AND ALEX FISCHER

COLONEL SAINT-GALON had just finished lunch. His orderly brought him a telegram. The Colonel read:

"In view of the approaching Grand Manœuvers, will come Saturday, three o'clock, to review your garrison.

LEQUÉPY DE CHÉNE,
General of the Brigade."

Without loss of a moment, Colonel de Saint-Galon sent for the four Commandants of the 199th of the Line.

"Dear friends," he announced to them, "I have just received a telegram from M. Lequépy de Chêne. He will come to review the garrison on Saturday . . . next Saturday . . . at . . ."

The Colonel hesitated for a moment. "I am on excellent terms with the General," mused he. "The day before yesterday he allowed me to offer him for his collection a ravishing sketch by Horace Vernet. It is evident that if he wished it, I can to-morrow be promoted General, I also. It is therefore of the greatest importance that the review of Saturday should be beyond criticism . . . Alas! I know them, those rascals! They are, as always, capable of not being ready at the time . . ."

"Yes, I was telling you," he pursued, "that M. Lequépy de Chêne will come on Saturday . . . Saturday . . . at . . . twelve, noon. Therefore at that hour your battalions must be assembled on the barrack square."

In great haste the four Commandants returned to their quarters. Without loss of a moment each of them sent for the four captains of his battalion.

"My friends," announced each of the Commandants to the four Captains under his orders, "I have this minute seen the Colonel. The General of the Brigade will review the garrison on Saturday . . . next Saturday . . . at . . . at . . ."

Each of the Commandants hesitated for a moment.

"I am on excellent terms with the Colonel. He allowed me last week to offer him a present of game. It is evident that if he wishes it, I can to-morrow be promoted Colonel, I also. It is therefore essential that I should offer to him an impeccable review . . . Alas! I know those lazy rascals! They are, as always, capable of . . ."

"Yes, I was telling you," resumed each of the Commandants, "that the General will come on Saturday . . . Saturday . . . at eight o'clock in the morning. Therefore at that hour your four Companies should be assembled on the barrack square."

In great haste the sixteen Captains returned to their quarters. Without loss of a moment each of them sent for the eight Lieutenants in his Company.

"Messieurs," declared each of the Captains to the eight Lieutenants under his orders. "I have this moment seen the Commandant. The General of the Brigade comes to review the garrison on Saturday . . . Saturday . . . at . . . at . . . at . . ."

Each of the sixteen Captains hesitated thirty seconds. "I am on excellent terms with my Commandant. He accepted my invitation to lunch ten days ago. It is evident that if he wishes it, I can to-morrow be promoted Commandant, I also. Attention that there is prepared for him a review of the best . . . Alas! I know them, those lascars! They are, as always . . ."

"Yes, I was telling you," resumed each of them, "that the General will come on Satur . . . No, Friday . . . yes, Friday . . . you hear, Friday at four o'clock in the afternoon. So at that hour I expect to see your eight platoons assembled on the barrack square."

In great haste the thirty-two lieutenants returned to the barracks. Without loss of a moment each of them got together the four Sergeants of his platoon.

"Now listen to what I have to say, you Sergeants. The General of the Brigade . . . I said the General of the Brigade himself . . . will come and review the garrison on Friday . . . Friday . . . at . . . at . . ."

Each of the thirty-two Lieutenants hesitated fifteen seconds. "Get on well with my Captain. Allowed me to offer him five vermouths this month. If he wishes it, can be a Captain to-morrow. Attention, Name of a Pipe, to get him up something worth

looking at . . . Alas! I know them, the swine! They
are . . ."

"Yes, the General will come on Friday, at ten
o'clock, you hear me, at ten o'clock in the morning.
See to it that at that hour your sections are all
assembled on the barrack square."

In great haste the one hundred and twenty-eight
Sergeants climbed the barrack staircase. Without
loss of a moment, each of them precipitated himself
into his room.

"Fall in there! . . . Keep your ears open, and
try to understand what you're going to be told. The
General . . . I said The GENERAL and not 'My
Cousin' . . . he's coming to review the garrison on
Friday . . ."

Each of the hundred and twenty-eight Sergeants
hesitated five seconds.

"Am in the good books of the Lieutenant. Let
me offer him two cigarettes on the march last month.
A word from him, and I'll be Sergeant-Major. Must
see to it, Bon Dieu, that I dish him up something
good . . . Alas! I know them like my own brother,
the dirty lot of shirkers! They . . ."

"Silence, Bon Dieu! I was telling you the General's coming here on Thursday . . . got that? . . .
Thursday . . . Thursday, Bon Sang de Bois . . .
Thursday at one o'clock in the afternoon. See to
it that your men are all out on the barrack square
at that time."

In great haste the four hundred and ninety-six
Corporals made for their rooms.

"Fall in! Get a move on, you squint-eyed blight-
ers! Silence! Nom de Dieu! Stand up! Look

out for yourselves! . . . The General of the Brigade
. . . didn't say the 'Canteen Sergeant' or old 'Mother
Jezebel' . . . he's coming to review the garrison on
Thursday . . ."

Each of the four hundred and ninety-six Corporals
hesitated half a second. "Sergeant's a pal o' mine.
Stood him half-a-pint three months ago. It's him
that gets the leave for you. No mistake about review
being a . . ."

"Shut your row, Tonerre de Brest! You loud-
mouthed blackguards . . . The General's coming
Thursday . . . yes, Thursday, to-morrow . . . to-
morrow morning! . . . At a quarter to five . . . No,
at half-past four, every man of you'll be on the barrack square! . . . Now, carry on! You've got no
time to waste!"

And this is why last Saturday the General of the
Brigade, Lequépy de Chêne—arriving moreover, at
the barracks of the 199th two hours late—muttered
incessantly to himself as he walked up and down
the ranks of the troops who, as the result of a so-
journ of three days and two nights on the barrack
square with rifles and packs, were even muddier than
the Grenadiers of Napoleon on their return from the
Russian Campaign:

"Are they not filthy, Saperlipopette! Are they
not disgusting, Saperlipopette de Saperlipopette!
You shall hear of this, Saint-Galon! Oh, I shall be
obliged to send in a pitiless report on the 199th,
Saint-Galon! It's sickening, positively sickening, to
see men in such a state!"

COLETTE WILLY

VI

GITANETTE

By Colette Willy

TEN o'clock. They have smoked so much in the Sémiramis Bar to-night that my compote of apples has a vague taste of Maryland tobacco. . . . It is Saturday. A touch of holiday fever animates the habituées, suggesting the joys of to-morrow, the happy day of do-nothing, the morning in bed followed by the excursion in a taxi to the Pavillion Bleu, the visit to relatives, the calling for children who are at some dreary school in the suburbs, and who will be brought, this beautiful Sunday, to breathe the pure air of the Châtelet . . .

The Sémiramis, crowded to overflowing, has prepared a monster soup-pot to serve as a massive base for the Sabbath dinner: "Thirty pounds of beef, my dear, and the giblets of six fowls! That ought to keep them quiet. An entrée for dinner and a salad for supper! and soup! They can have as much soup as they can hold!" Her mind at ease, the proprietress smokes her eternal cigarette, smiling like a kindly ogress as she passes from table to table, sipping mechanically the whisky-and-soda she carries in her hand. Coffee, bitter and strong, is growing cold in my cup; my dog, sneezing with the smoke, keeps begging me to go . . .

"Don't you remember me?" says a voice close to me.

A young woman in black, very simply, almost poorly dressed, is looking questioningly at me. She has dark hair that hardly shows under the brim of her black straw hat with its two knife feathers, a white collar, a little cravat, and soiled light gray gloves . . .

Powder, rouge on the lips, blackened eyelids, the indispensable make-up, but it has been laid on with a careless hand, by necessity, by habit. I reflect, and suddenly, the beautiful large eyes, of a brown-black that shine like the Sémiramis coffee, remind me:

"But it's Gitanette!"

Her name, her absurd music-hall name, comes back to me with the memory of how we met.

Three or four years ago when I was playing in a sketch at the Empyrée, Gitanette occupied a little dressing-room next to mine. Gitanette and her friend, a pair of "cosmopolitan dancers," dressed there, their door open on to the corridor to let in the air . . . Gitanette was generally dressed like a boy, and her Friend—Rita? Lina? Nina?—appeared turn by turn as some fantastic character, an Italian, in high boots as a Cossack, draped in a Spanish shawl with a carnation behind her ear . . . A nice little couple who did not hide their devotion to one another; Gitanette was the leading spirit, and she showed an almost maternal authority in the way she took care of her friend . . . The friend, Nina, Rita, or Lina, I have almost forgotten. Hair dyed golden, bright eyes, white teeth, something in the style of a young washer-woman, appetizing and untrustworthy.

They danced neither well nor badly, and their history was that of most "Dance Numbers." It is young, supple, it is sick of the bar, full of women, and the promenade, so it saves all its poor little coppers to pay so much a week to a ballet-master and a costumier ... And if it has extraordinary luck, it begins to get little engagements in Paris, in the provinces, and abroad ...

Gitanette and her friend, then, were "doing a turn" at the Empyrée that month. For thirty evenings they showed me the discreet and disinterested attentions, the kind reserve and courtesy that you frequently find behind the scenes in a music-hall. At the moment when I was putting the last touch of rouge under my eyelids, they would run, their foreheads moist, their mouths trembling from shortness of breath, smiling without speaking because they were panting like the ponies that used to turn the round-about at fairs. When they had a little recovered, by way of "good evening" they would tell me politely that the house was full and in a good temper, or: "There's no pleasing them to-night!"

Then before undressing herself, Gitanette would unlace the bodice of her friend, throwing over her shoulders a kimono of printed cotton to keep her from getting a chill, and the little animal, Rita, Nina, or Lina, who always looked a little debauched, would begin to laugh and chatter and swear: "Be very careful," she would call to me, "the roller-skaters have cut into the floor, and it's difficult not to find yourself on your nose to-night!"

The voice of Gitanette, quiet and grave, would reply: "It's good luck to have a tumble ... It's

a sign you'll do a turn again in the house before
three years are out. It was like that when I was
dancing at the Bouffes at Bordeaux; I caught my
foot in a . . ."

They lived out aloud, as it were, beside me, their
door wide open. They made little bird-like noises,
full of their dancing and their affection for each
other, happy to work together, to take refuge in
each other, protected one by the other from the men
who hang round music halls, from what might easily
lead to dreary prostitution . . .

All this comes back to me as I look at this sad and
lonely Gitanette, so changed.

"Sit down a moment, Gitanette, let's have some
coffee together . . . And . . . your friend, where
is she?"

She sits down, shakes her head:

"We aren't together any longer, my friend and me.
You haven't heard what happened?"

"No, I haven't heard anything . . . Is it indis-
creet to ask you?"

"No! Oh, no! You, you are an artist, like me
. . . that is, like I used to be, because now I am
nothing. I'm not even a woman . . ."

"It's as grave as that?"

"Grave—that depends on what you call grave.
It depends on your nature. My nature's the sort
that attaches itself. I attached myself to Rita; she
was everything in the world to me; I never, never
thought it could change. . . . The year that it happened we'd been having a great success. We hadn't
finished dancing at the Apollo when Salomon, the
agent, wrote to us, and we got engaged to dance in

the revue at the Empyrée, a magnificent revue, twelve
hundred costumes, English girls, everything. I didn't
much care about it; I was always afraid of revues
where there are a lot of women; it leads to disputes
and rivalries and scandal. At the end of a fortnight
of the revue I was wishing we were back doing our
little turns by ourselves. And soon I was longing
for it, for there was my little Rita changing towards
me, thinking of nothing but being with the others,
with a new friendship here and a new friendship
there, and soon she was always having champagne
in Lucie Desrosier's dressing-room, a fat, red-headed
lump who stank of brandy, and always wore corsets
with the bones broken . . . Champagne at twenty-
three sous the bottle. I ask you whether you can get
anything good at that price! . . . My Rita grew
quarrelsome and very hard to deal with. One evening what did she do but come into the dressing-room
and tell me some one had been making love to her!
I ask whether that was the right sort of way to
behave to me? I grew more and more miserable,
and everything seemed wrong. I'd have given anything to have got an engagement at Hamburg, or in
the Winter Garten at Berlin, so as to get away
from that revue which seemed to be going on for
ever!"

Gitanette turns towards me her beautiful coffee-
colored eyes; they are full of pain, and all the life
has gone out of them.

"I'm telling you exactly how things were, you
understand. Don't imagine that I'm inventing or
speaking maliciously!"

"Certainly not, Gitanette!"

"That's right. Well, one day my bad little Rita came to me and said: 'Look here, Gitanette, I want a petticoat'—they wore petticoats that year—'and a nice one; I'm ashamed of mine.' Of course it was always me who took care of the money, or else we shouldn't have had food to eat! . . . I asked her how much it would cost. 'How much, how much!' she shouted to me, 'you'd think I hadn't the right to buy myself a petticoat!' So as not to have a scene, I just said: 'Here's the key, take what you need, but don't forget we have to pay the month for our room to-morrow!' She took a fifty-franc note, and flung her clothes on anyhow, because she said she wanted to be at the Galeries Lafayette before the shop grew crowded. I sat down to mend and do up two costumes that had just come from the cleaners, and I sewed and I sewed as I waited for her . . . It was getting late when I found that I should have to get some *mousseline de soie* to make a new frill for a lining to one of Rita's costumes, and I rushed out to try and get it before the shop shut . . . Just telling you about it makes me see it all as if it was happening at this very minute. As I hurried out of the shop, I was almost run over by a taxi that drew up at the curb, and what did I see? The fat Desrosiers getting out of it, untidy and hot, and waving her hand to Rita, to my Rita, who was sitting in the taxi! . . . My head went round, and I almost fell down, and when I felt better, and would have called out to Rita, the taxi had gone, taking Rita back to our room . . .

"I went home dazed; of course she was there, Rita. And what a face she had! . . . you want to know her as I do to understand a face like that . . .

"It won't stand thinking about . . .

"I couldn't find anything to say except: 'And your petticoat?' 'I haven't bought one.' 'And the fifty francs?' 'I lost it.' She said that looking in my eyes, and her eyes . . . But you can't imagine it . . . you can't understand . . ."

Her eyes lowered, Gitanette feverishly turns her spoon in her cup . . .

"It was like a knife in my chest, hearing those words. It was as if I had been there and seen it all myself, the rides in the taxi, the meeting, the visit to the bed-sitting-room with champagne on the table, all, all . . ."

Beneath her breath she keeps on repeating: "All . . . all . . ." till I interrupt her with a:

"And what did you do?"

"Nothing. I cried all through dinner into my plate of mutton and beans . . . And then, a week afterwards, she left me. And *fortunately* I fell ill, dangerously ill, because if I hadn't, in spite of loving her as I did, I should have gone and killed her . . ."

She speaks quietly of killing and dying, still turning the spoon in her cold coffee. This simple-minded girl, who lives so near to nature, knows that just one action, easy, nothing violent about it, is all that is necessary to ease her sufferings . . . To be dead, to be alive, it is all the same, except that you can choose death, whereas you can't choose life . . .

"Did you want to die, Gitanette?"

"Of course I did," she says. "Only I was so ill, I couldn't. And when I came out of hospital, my grandmother took me with her and looked after me while I was getting well. She's very old, and now I feel I oughtn't to leave her . . ."

"Besides, you are getting over it now, aren't you?"

"No," says Gitanette in a low voice. "And I don't want to. I don't want to feel less miserable. I should be ashamed to console myself with any one else after having loved her so much. Perhaps you'll say as the others do: 'Amuse yourself . . . time changes everything . . .' I know that time changes most things, but that depends on the person. I've never had any one to love except Rita; it's just happened like that; I never had a friend; I never knew what it was to be a child, because my parents died when I was a baby, but when I've seen lovers happy together, or fathers and mothers with their little children on their knees, I used to say: 'I have all that they have, because I've got Rita!' And now that I've lost her, my life is finished; there's nothing to be done. Whenever I go to my grandmother's, into my room, and see the photographs of Rita, our photographs in all our turns, and the little dressing-table where we both used to do our hair, every time I go in, it all begins over again, and I cry, and I talk to her, and I call her . . . It makes me ill, but somehow I like it. It is a funny thing to say, but it seems to me that I shouldn't know what to do if I wasn't miserable like that. It seems to keep me company."

LUCIE DELARUE-MADRUS

VII

THE INHERITANCE

By LUCIE DELARUE-MADRUS

HE did not possess any of the things that make for happiness, and he was not happy. Undersized and ugly, he had never been loved, nor had he ever loved any one.

Left an orphan at an early age, his parents having died in a distant country where business had taken them, he had been brought up by strangers who had got rid of him as soon as they could. An insignificant employee in an insignificant office, morose, poor and alone, by the time he was thirty he had come to the conclusion that the life of certain beings is an offense to commonsense, and tired of his mediocrity, sick of the monotony of his existence, his thoughts turned to suicide.

Now, thoughts of suicide suggest many possibilities. The man who can see the insignificance of life cannot be quite insignificant. As a matter of fact, Paul had been born with a capacity for passionate tenderness and for action, but circumstances had stifled these undeveloped characteristics. Timid, he was too diffident to look for love; modest, he lacked the self-confidence that would have invented for him the ambition which is an active form of hope. He

was like a beggar who waits for the alms that do not
come because he does not hold out his hand.

It happened, therefore, that the idea of voluntary
death awakened something that had hitherto slept
in the depths of his sluggish mind. The thoughts
that rose in him were bitter, but they produced a
kind of mental intoxication. He felt something of
the exultation that animates poets and lovers. To
die! The idea lifted him above the drab, unevent-
ful days and nights, filled the colorless hours with
a somber lyricism.

While his fellow-workers were writing the love-
letters they kept hidden between the sheets of their
blotting-paper, he sat wondering which would be the
best way to put an end to himself. There was no.
one he wished to impress, so he did not waste time
in considering picturesque methods, concentrating in--
stead on trying to imagine which would be the quick-
est and most comfortable manner, entailing the least
suffering, and sparing him fear of the action.

He was much impressed by the details of a little
tragedy he read one morning in the newspaper, and
he decided that skilful hanging, with its sudden
breaking of the vertebræ, would produce instant
death.

"I will give myself eight days," he thought, "to
get used to the idea."

He knew that certain poisons would have a more
rapid result. But how could he procure them?

About the seventh day the men in his office began
to notice that there was some change in him. He
had the look of some one sickening for an illness, but
no one suspected that it was an "illness" that meant

death next night. No remark was made to him, partly because one does not make such comments, but chiefly because no one cared whether he was ill or well. Paul had no more interest for them than the stove or the high stool; less, because the stove warmed them in winter, and the stool was useful when they had to reach up for books on the top shelves.

The eighth day came, and as Paul went to business in the morning, he stopped at a shop and bought a cord. He put it in his pocket, and arrived at the office with nervous shiverings that made his teeth chatter.

"He's going to get influenza, and we shall all catch it," thought the others angrily.

He walked home very slowly that night. His concierge greeted him with a grumble; she prepared his evening meal, the only one he had at home, and he was late.

"Don't worry," he said. "I don't want anything to eat to-night . . ."

The nervous shiver returned as he reflected that these were the last words he would speak on earth, and that they were as insignificant as his life. But as he mounted the staircase, the woman came running after him.

"I'd forgotten," she said. "Here's a letter for you."

A letter? . . . He took it with a feeling of astonishment that made him for a moment almost forget his approaching death.

When he had lit the lamp, he opened it. At first he failed to grasp its meaning. A solicitor? . . .

A cousin who had just died? . . . He had not known that he possessed any relatives. He read the letter over again, and an ironic smile crept over his face as he realized that it told him that an inheritance had come to him from his unknown family, and that the inheritance was—a vault in Père Lachaise where there was one last vacant place at his disposal!

The coincidence seemed too striking to be possible, and as he tried to realize it, new thoughts, complicated and obscure, passed through his mind.

The Pharaohs of Egypt had their tombs constructed during their lifetime, and visited them frequently out of respect for their own images which were buried there in advance. Paul knew nothing of all that, but he became possessed with an ardent desire to see this last habitation that destiny had offered him in such an extraordinary manner.

"Let me see . . . to-day is Friday. I will wait till Sunday night. On Sunday afternoon I will go and see it."

When at last he stood before his vault, his first sensation was one of unexpected pride.

Large, and covered by a handsome chapel, it seemed to him very beautiful, and all at once he felt himself important, almost rich. Certainly comparatively few people could expect to have such a sepulcher.

Curiosity as to who were to be his companions in the eternal sleep then moved him to read the names. The last-comer, a very recent inmate, he from whom the inheritance had come, and who had not even suspected the existence of this poor relative, had the same name as himself, Paul.

He read the age: fifty years.

"That's not old . . ."

Leaning against the little iron gate of the vault, his eyes eager with curiosity, he reflected:

"He must have been all alone in life just as I am, seeing that the lawyers had to look so long to find me . . ."

Alone in life, yes, but not in death . . . He read the other names.

"This is my family," he thought, and the idea of having people of his own seemed to open a new world to him. Something tender rose in him, giving him a sense of happiness such as he had never before felt. His imagination came into play, and he tried to see the faces, to invent biographies.

"My cousin Estelle; died when she was eighteen. . . . My cousin Charles: ninety years old . . ."

When he went home that evening he looked without conviction at the cord. After all why should a man go out of his way to kill himself when it was quite certain he would die some day. The sight of his beautiful burial-place, full of his own dead, had made him aware of the value and the power of life.

"I—I stand up straight! I can talk; I can walk; my eyes can see. I—I breathe."

A kind of triumphant pity made his heart beat fast. Living, he was superior to all that sleeping family; he was their master, their lord.

"Next Sunday I will go again and take them some flowers . . ."

In future there would be somewhere to go on Sunday afternoons. He no longer felt isolated, alone in the world. He had a strange, mysterious home-circle of his own.

He sat down at the table to answer the solicitor's letter. The neat bundle of new cord was before him, and he pushed it aside, almost without noticing it, as he stretched out his hand for a sheet of writing paper.

LUCIEN DESCAVES

VIII

THE DAY OUT

By LUCIEN DESCAVES

BETRAYED, and soon to be a mother—fatal result of a public ball in her native town—Florentine had come, like so many others, to Paris to conceal the living witness of her downfall. She was received into the Maternity Hospital. When she left it, she did so with a fixed resolution.

To return to her own town with her infant was not to be thought of. Nor could she gain the immediate and substantial means of livelihood which a situation as wet-nurse would have procured for her; she was not able to feed her own child. There was nothing for it but to leave the baby temporarily with the Assistance Publique; and when she had signed the crude form of abandon, she found herself standing in the street with empty arms, her face scalded with tears.

She repeated to herself the last replies of the clerk to her reiterated question: "And it's quite sure that when I am in a position to take her back they will let me have her?"

"Certainly."

"And while I am waiting they will let me know how she gets on?"

"Yes, every three months at the Avenue Victoria.

Show them this, and you will get the information you require."

And he had slipped into her hand a little bit of paper like an omnibus ticket.

Never would she forget her first visit to that Information Department.

Three women preceded her in the narrow corridor that ended in a sort of grille. She had not long to wait. A clerk took the numbers, turned over the leaves of a register, and dismissed the women, one after another, with the single word: "Living."

There was only one more before Florentine, a young girl, bareheaded, her clothes tattered. She showed her ticket timidly, and her humble eyes followed the clerk feverishly as he turned over the pages.

At last he raised his head and said: "Dead."

She stared, gaping, stunned, hoping—hoping what? That there was some mistake? For particulars? For the name of the disease of which it had died? The place where it was buried? . . .

It was now Florentine's turn, and the clerk, like an automaton, said: "Living."

Florentine persisted: "You are sure she is not ill?"
Silence.

"Please tell me where I can write to find out?"

The clerk saw he had a novice to deal with and to get rid of her he explained: "We are not allowed to give details. Your child is alive: that's the chief thing."

She returned every three months on the day specified on the ticket. Her heart used to beat furiously as she approached the grille, showed her credentials, and scrutinized the impassive face of the clerk to try and read there the word that would put an end to her sickening suspense.

"Living!" She no longer put any further questions, and went away with a heart full of unspeakable gratitude. It was the torture and the joy of the only outing she ever asked of her employers. Without relations, with no friends to go and see, and no money to spend, why should she want to go out? She avoided all expense that was not absolutely necessary, trying to put by a little hoard that would eventually enable her to assume the duties of maternity. But in two years she was only able to save sixty francs. She was not strong, and twice she had to go to hospital. She came out looking ill and incapable, and the registry offices never sent her to any but poor places where, more often than not, she was treated as a slave.

But at last these hardships came to an end. She found a situation where there were breathing-spaces, moments of rest, and she could recruit her strength. A simple old couple, quiet and considerate; very little hard work; fair wages. A real haven of rest. And Florentine was at last able to put aside the money that meant getting possession of her daughter.

Then came the date for the visit, for going "to see her" as she called it. Madame willingly granted the request for the day out, the more readily as Florentine promised to be back in time to prepare dinner. She kept her word; at five o'clock she was bending over the pans on the kitchen range. But at table Madame was puzzled and inquisitive:

"Have you noticed how upset Florentine seems?

She'd got her apron up to her face when I went into the kitchen just now. Something must have gone wrong with her when she was out . . ."

"Perhaps her sapper has turned to another and a fairer," said the old gentleman, whose pleasantries dated from the second Empire.

"Or perhaps her fireman hasn't come up to scratch," corrected Madame, who was more up-to-date.

They watched the girl stealthily, growing excited when they saw that the expression of her face had quite changed. The cooking was very bad.

"The soup was much too salt—she must have been crying into it!" said Monsieur wittily.

Madame agreed, adding mischievously:

"It's been the same with all the courses. Everything has tasted of tears to-night."

HENRI DUVERNOIS

IX

THE FEZ

By Henri Duvernois

NISSIM remembered that he had once been a Turk chiefly because, long ago, it was with a fez on his head that he used to walk the pavement outside the cafés selling snow-white rahat-loukoum and chunks of nougat in which the almonds looked like yellow teeth set awry in discolored gums. Happy, care-free days of juvenile commerce! Armed with a platter of highly-burnished copper and a damascened spoon, he had wandered through the world, beguiling the frau, the miss, the señora, teaching them the insipid delights of his sugary wares—and of other things, as opportunity presented itself. Serious, too, in spite of his perpetual smile and the engaging twinkle in his eyes. And with all the more respect for the authorities because he had no civil status; was not even sure where he came from. Hunger had driven him away when he was quite a child from the hovel where too many lousy little brothers and sisters with ringworm had scrambled about in the dust. But now he had realized his ambition, and was in Paris; his hair was turning gray, as was also his big mustache; he spoke a weird language composed of the slang of all the countries through which he had wandered, but it

was softened by a natal accent that gave a softened
song-like effect to all he said.

He explored the terraces of the Parisian cafés
with a queer old top-hat on his head; his frock-coat
and trousers were brown, and he wore a big white
necktie, patent boots, and an air of jovial dignity
like that of the notary of vaudeville. He carried in
his hand a sample-box, one of those used by jewel-
ers' travelers, in which were rings with three pearls
set trefoil-fashion, and a diamond in the middle to
represent a drop of dew, souvenir brooches, and out-
of-date medallions. And every pocket concealed a
watch with a double case, which he would open and
turn about before the dazzled client.

"Better than gold, monsié."

And if "monsié" betrayed the least interest, he
would deliberately take a chair, sit down, and open
his box with a "Phuuu!" that suggested that he had
wonders to reveal, nor would he spare the hoped-
for client the inspection of one single compartment.
He exhibited his trinkets with grace; his hand
stretched like a pigeon's wing as he placed a brooch
on madame's neck, or slipped a ring on her finger,
nor did he forget to take from his pocket, by way of
interlude, the plain watch suitable for an ordinary
person, or the splendid chronometer fit for a gallant,
with an enamel picture on the back showing a lady
of Montmartre enjoying a bottle of champagne.

"That, that all what is very best, monsié."

At midnight he would return to his room on the
sixth floor in the rue du Helder, for he had at last
succeeded in making a little fatherland for himself
near the boulevards where he gained his living. In

the summer, during the dead season, he remained there, showing his wares, just for the pleasure of doing it, to the municipal water-cart man, to the flower-sellers, to the police.

He knew nobody except Bichon, Mademoiselle Bichon of the café-concerts, who came sometimes to see him when she was in need of money. A terrible Bichon, somewhere about forty, more plastered with powder than his rahat-loukoum, but infinitely less sweet. He adored her, and watched her with fear, for she did not scruple to help herself from his sample-case, taking from it a ring, a brooch, a chain, just as she would pick grapes from a bunch on a plate. For eighteen years she had crushed him with her reproaches, threats, cruelties, lies and betrayals. He had given her a key of his room, and she came whenever she liked. The concierge would warn Nissim:

"Go up quickly. Your Camel is waiting for you."

And Nissim was so conciliating, so amiable, so anxious to please every one—the habit of his trade— he would sometimes ask his door-keeper:

"Monsieur Parentier, has not Madame my Camel ask for me?"

But as soon as he had opened his door, he would stoop down to murmur to Bichon, huddled up in an uneasy doze:

"It is me, my dove, do not be disturbed."

Over and over again she had bidden him a last good-by with a fierce joy, setting out for tours that were supposed to bring her money and fame, but from which she returned still thinner and more evil-tempered, her hair limp, her mouth bitter because

she had sung to a chorus of insults. He would bow
his head, overjoyed to see her again, the slave of
his love——he who came of a race where the women
are slaves, bewitched by this vixen whose feet he
kissed with devotion, letting her rob him without
protest, torture him without a word of complaint.
All that was beautiful seemed to resemble her, from
the goddesses on his brooches to the dancers in
enamel drinking champagne on the back of his best
watches.

One night on returning home he found her in bed,
and trembled with joy. He had believed her lost,
far away in some remote part of Europe, and here
she was back from a three-weeks' absence in Orleans.

She received his expression of joy with a question:

"What the devil are you doing here?"

He started, taken aback by the question. She
explained:

"I'm asking what the devil you are doing here
while your brothers are all out there fighting?"

He tried to take it as a joke.

"Ah! the war? I too old, my dove, and all that
is politics: me, I sell my little jewelry; I not think
of other things . . ."

"Are you a Turk? Yes or no?"

"I not a Turk. I seller of jewelry."

"Then you don't read the papers?"

He shook his head. The papers cost money, and
besides, he could scarcely read at all. In any case,
this sort of conversation had no interest for him;
he wanted to find Bichon in the kindly mood which
sometimes preluded a request for a hat or a pair of
boots. But she insisted:

"But where do you come from?"

He reflected. It was so long since he had left his birth-place. Finally he pronounced a name, barbarous and soft of sound. In that far-off land there was sunshine and blue sky, but so much poverty, so much misery. He imagined himself back there, running about in a dirty shirt and scrambling among the dogs for food.

"They never hurt me . . . I liked them . . . Once I cried. The mother-dogs had put their puppies safe in a hole in a big dust-heap . . . and the big rain came, and all the little dogs were drowned. We not have toys there; we play with what we found. So we play with the little dead dogs, but we cried, and cried . . ."

He shook himself and squared his shoulders. What connection could there possibly be between that starved urchin and this gentleman peddler with his case of jewelry, his frock-coat, his high hat, the real tradesman that he had become, living in rue du Helder, surrounded by his own furniture, and with a magnificent sweetheart with yellow hair?

"Kiss Nissim and not talk politics," he urged. "Not like to talk of poor beggars . . ."

"You'd shake with fright if they made you go and fight! How old are you?"

He made a vague gesture. He didn't know. He didn't know anything about himself. He was Nissim and that was all. He used to sell sweet-meats out in the big world; now he was tired, hungering for cossetings and rest; he thought of nothing but his trade and Bichon. She must not ask too much of him. He tapped his forehead with his fist.

"An old animal, my dove, Nissim an old, old animal who loves you . . ."

But to-night his cajoleries were without effect; his smile had lost its brilliance, and his eyes, the eyes dimmed by the electric glare of cafés, wearied by having implored attention from too many people, begged instead of fascinating.

"You don't even know that your country is at war. Wait a minute!"

She got up. Her face wore its expression of bad days, and her movements had the quickness that only came when she was on the point of playing one of her worst tricks.

"I've brought you the papers; I'm going to read them to you."

Resigning himself to this incomprehensible caprice, he sat down, his hat still on his head, his sample-case on his knees, his elbows pressed close to his sides so that he could protect the watches if she pushed violently against him. She picked up some newspapers she had brought, and spread them out on the table.

"They're getting it hot; your Turks! Wait a moment and you'll see."

He looked at her uneasily—surely it would have been better to lie down and fall happily asleep, thinking of nothing but each other! But she kept to her idea, and began to read. An immense respect for her took possession of him as he listened, the respect of the ignorant for those who can read. How clever she was, this Bichon! And what a pretty voice she had . . .

Then, all of a sudden, he understood. It was the account of a terrible defeat: rifles thrown away in heaps, death, terror, the cholera, hunger—above all, hunger, the Turkish hunger that he had known. And at the recollection his stomach turned.

"They're getting it hot! They're getting it hot!" repeated Bichon with frenzied joy.

Corpses . . . prisoners . . . no alleviation for the agony of the wounded; Death without Glory. The names of the towns taken one by one touched some vague note of remembrance in the awakening brain of Nissim. He had heard those names before, long ago; he repeated them to himself under his breath: "Bonnar Hissar . . . Karagatch . . . Viza . . ."

When she had finished, Bichon raised her head. Nissim still had his case on his knees, but he was trembling convulsively. Never had Bichon seen a man tremble like that. It almost alarmed her.

"Are you ill?"

He trembled still more violently. She was beginning to laugh scornfully:

"Oh! Mountebanks like you . . ."

But Nissim was standing, drawn up to his full height before her, and suddenly fear seized her. Up in his little room on the sixth floor of the rue du Helder, Nissim had in a flash become filled with the poignant distress, the impotent rage, of the vanquished who had fallen in that distant land. But he was so young when he left his country. Hadn't he said so himself just now? He didn't remember anything at all about it; he had said it was "all politics." But she saw she had made a mistake. She ought not to have spoken like that; it would have been better to have gone to bed at once, not to have brought up such a distressing subject. And she asked him to forgive her for having laughed. But he pushed her hat and dress towards her.

"Quick! Quick! Get out."

Panic-stricken, she dressed in haste. In five minutes the old idiot had relapsed into a Turk! He was throwing her out as he would have thrown her out of a harem. She fled, banging the door behind her with an oath.

Nissim was alone. He rummaged in a trunk, and got out his fez, the fez he wore when he sold rahat-loukoum and nougat. It was all moth-eaten, but he threw his high hat aside, and put it on his head. Then, some irresistible force made him bow his head; words, soft and barbarous, rose to his lips, words he had used as a little child, full of sunshine, of odors, and of suffering, words of whose meaning he knew nothing, except that they formed a prayer.

And he fell on his knees sobbing—his face turned towards Mecca.

CLAUDE FARRÉRE

X

THE TURRET

By Claude Farrere

FARGUE, naval lieutenant, gunnery specialist, officer of the fore-turret A, takes a firm grip with both hands on the rungs of the rope-ladder and climbs to the steel ladder. When he reaches the trap-door, he secures himself with one hand and pushes with the other; the trap-door opens with a great clanging of ironwork. A voice from above calls out:

"Attention!"

Fargue mounts the last three rungs, raises himself on his wrists, and finally sets foot on the iron flooring. The door falls back, closing the trap. The crews are drawn up in perfect order on each side of the guns: heels together, right hands at the salute, left hands by their sides.

"Stand easy!" Fargue orders.

Then making his way between the guns, he perches himself on the officer's seat to see what is happening outside. Nothing out of the ordinary is to be seen through the holes in the sighting-board. As far as the eye can reach, the gray seas are breaking in long parallel lines of foam, and the battleships are moving "in line ahead" through these breaking seas, each one following in the wake of the ship ahead.　Fargue makes a half-turn and steps down again to the deck to make an inspection before the practice begins.

His warrant-officer smiles cordially in greeting.

"Morning, Gourvès. . . . Anything to report to-day?"

"Nothing at all, sir."

"Have you adjusted the training-gear?"

"Yes, sir."

"There is not too much slack in the driving-chains?"

"We took up a link this morning.　It is now exactly the length you showed us last time."

"Good."

Fargue moves over to the armor-plated side and leans against it . . .

To-day there is every prospect of protracted manœuvers: they will pretend to engage a hostile fleet, represented by their own light cruisers.　Doubtless, with a scheme affording such infinite opportunities for the most unforeseen fantasies on the part of the Admirals, they will have a taste of everything, and find out what it means "to dig holes in the waves."　But what is the use of tiring oneself beforehand?　So Fargue, leaning up against the wall, runs his eye over his turret.

. . . A two-gun turret with twelve-inch armor-plating—what a beautiful thing!　Just try to imagine an oval room about twenty-three feet long and nineteen feet broad, with a very low ceiling, and all made of polished steel.　Inside it are two prodigious guns, lying side by side, two guns whose long barrels jut out forty feet beyond the turret through the double

embrasure, and whose breeches are so large as to fill
the turret to such an extent that one wonders, at first
sight, where the thirteen men, who are required for
working them, can possibly find room.   Yet they
manage to do so, and their presence does not seem
to add materially to the indescribable congestion of
the place.   As for the guns, they hardly count!
There are the recoil cylinders, the slides, the cradles;
the ammunition hoists, the ammunition cages, the
sighting-gear, the elevating cylinders, the telescopes,
the turn-table, the gun carriages and the projectile
rails; the rammers, the sponges, the wash-out gear,
the hydraulic-pipe system, the air-service and the
electric system . . . there is an inextricably tangled
mass of iron, steel, copper and brass; there are trains
of cog-wheels which the thirteen men, cogs of another
sort, but more perfected and no less disciplined, work
with the greatest method and meticulous care—it is
fine!   The roof does not lie directly on the walls: a
row of steel supports, like a colonnade, separates
them, forming a series of horizontal loopholes, an
inch or so high, between the roof and the walls, by
which the sea-breeze can penetrate, tempered by the
sun-warmed daylight; and this daylight is supple-
mented by the cold light of the electric lamps.   The
result is that you can see well enough.   It is fine!
Through this sort of cornice made of daylight, the
thirteen men can also, from time to time, as the ship
rolls, get a glimpse outside and find out what is
going on.

    There are thirteen of them: the second-in-com-
mand, keeping an eye on the whole apparatus, is the
brain: the two petty officers, each in charge of a gun,

the motor nerves: the two certificated gunlayers, the eyes: the two extra gunlayers, spare eyes: the two loaders and the two ammunition providers, the muscles: one armorer, the healing faculty: and lastly, the officer, the soul. Thirteen men and yet they are but one: one entity composed of their thirteen beings —the turret, the forward turret, the twin turret with twelve-inch armor-plating, the most awesome weapon of offense on the battleship, her best and surest means of issuing victorious from battles to come.

*   *   *   *   *   *   *

It has begun. Outside, the roll of the drums, followed by two single strokes, means: "Load!" Fargue stands up and gives the word: "Close up!" and immediately perches himself on the officer's seat. Far away over the misty sea, striped zebra-wise with lines of foam on green water, he can see through the slits of his sighting-hood some confused silhouettes rising over the horizon: the light squadron, the cruisers that represent the hostile fleet. Fargue looks round to make sure that each of the personnel is standing immovable in his appointed place, and gives out, one after the other, the necessary orders. "Raise the cages!" "Load!" "Close the breeches!" After which, his eyes fixed on the receivers, he himself waits until the bridge gives him, in turn, his orders, the supreme will of the Admiral, transmitted through the Captain, who is at his post up there in the conning-tower.

Meanwhile the breech blocks clang, the loading trays fall back, the ammunition hoists rumble as the ratchets click. Of course they do not really put charges in the guns; they only pretend to do so; but all the motions are gone through as if they were real shells and real charges which they were ramming at top speed into the open, well-oiled barrels. Gourvès, the warrant-officer, takes out his watch to time the operation. . . . No. 1 gun "loads" well: its petty-officer, Le Kellec, is a good man, with plenty of "go" in him, and reliable . . . Twenty-three seconds! Splendid! Why! that's equal to record time! not a fifth of a second over! . . . No. 2 is behindhand: Fontan is not so good a man as Le Kellec. . . . Gourvès shrugged his shoulders in scorn: as for Fontan, a Dago from Dagoland, can you expect him to be as good as a Breton? A Breton from Mor-laix? A Le Kellec from Gourvès' own part of the country? Gourvès would be angry enough to kill Fontan if he should ever "get into the same street" with Le Kellec. All the same, too long is too long: thirty-four seconds—that necessitates a bit of slang-ing.

"Now, then, wake up there, Fontan! Has your crew gone to sleep, and you with them?"

Fontan does not move an eyelash; but near him an irritated click of the tongue gives answer to the reproof. No doubt about where that comes from! It is Brénéol, the loader, with his "back-chat." He is given to "backchat," is Brénéol! Not a bad gun-ner except for that. The only thing to do is to close one's ears. If one chooses to hear—well, one would be obliged to punish, and what good would that do? Gourvès does not hear; Fargue does not hear either.

For they are men, these thirteen cog-wheels of

the turret; men like you and me; and it is only here, in the turret, that they are cog-wheels. Anywhere else the difference in their birth, their nationality, their instincts, education, habits, outlook, and their brains render them as different as you, doubtless, are from me. Take Le Kellec and Fontan—when off duty do you imagine that they ever exchange one single word? And Brénéol, the loader, taciturn and stubborn; and Le Duc, the gunlayer of No. 2 gun, a well-behaved lad; and Tiphaigne, the reserve gunlayer, an anarchist, who inserts the last copy of the *Libertaire* into his text-book on naval gunnery, so that he can read either class of literature in the hours devoted to the study of theory; and Penven who hands out the ammunition, always drunk from the moment he sets foot on shore, where he lives in the lowest localities; and Brazière, the armorer, a Bachelor of Science, who prefers soiling his white hands with oil and rust to being a nonentity in some college; and Lohéac d'Elfe, the gunlayer of No. 1, who is of noble birth, and was once rich, but has chosen to enlist, no one knows why . . . do you imagine that they consort together and become intimate, men like this who probably have not three ideas in common? No! Emphatically NO! Each one "sets his own course," and silently follows his own particular ideas in his own way, keeping away from those who would disturb his peace. It is only here, behind the armor-plate, under this low roof, on this resonant floor, that all-powerful discipline knits these different natures together, coördinates them, molds them, kneads them until they form one living entity—the Turret . . .

Fargue falls into a reflective mood, and puts this question to himself: What is it really worth, this indispensable discipline? To what degree does it influence them? How strongly does it bind them together, remodel them in its melting pot? To what point can one rely on this human metal? It can never be decided until war comes and takes them close to Death, facing Death, the supreme touchstone . . .

*   *   *   *   *   *   *

"Close up!"

A bell sounds. The needles on the receiver-board change their position. Fargue issues his orders:

"Bearing eighty degrees! Train right, third speed! . . . Range, eight thousand six hundred! Deflection, thirty-two thousandths, left . . . On the first cruiser from the left! Ready! . . ."

The order is already carried out. The turret pivots round, smoothly and quickly. Through the sighting slits, Fargue watches the horizon as it passes under his view. There are the cruisers slipping along in Indian file from starboard to port, like fantastic Chinese silhouettes. The rest of the men, standing on tiptoe, look also, and take in the situation.

The battleships are steaming in "line ahead" parallel to the "line ahead" of the cruisers. The battleships, in splendid order, at four hundred mètres interval, are each steering just to the right of the stern of the preceding vessel. This presents a double view of long gliding hulls and clean-cut masts under the ensigns fluttering in the breeze . . .

"Independent firing! . . . Commence! . . ."

Several reports have rung out; they are blank rounds fired by the Admiral as a sort of warning signal. The cruisers over there are now aware that fire has been opened on them.

"Eight thousand mètres! . . . Seven thousand six hundred! . . . Seven thousand four hundred! . . ."

The crews briskly work the handles of the laying and training gear. Ha! Is the enemy coming nearer to us? Probably the "boss" is slanting on to the light squadron, on the sly, without seeming to do so. . . . Well, it's their look-out if they don't take the hint. They are not powerful enough to join issue at short range. Le Kellec, with a rapid glance through the loopholes, estimates the variation of the range. Brazière, his hands on his hips, is busy calculating the cosine of the angle of approach. Tephaigne chuckles to himself, and thinks of universal disarmament. Penven lets his thoughts wander to women. Lohéac d'Elfe, as usual unaffected by anything, verifies his line of aim . . .

The bell tinkles again. Fargue gives fresh orders.

"Same target! . . . Bearing, zero degrees! . . . Train left, third speed! . . . Range, seven thousand eight hundred! . . . eight thousand two hundred! . . . eight thousand four hundred! . . . Deflection, six left! . . . Continue the firing! . . ."

So they are not so stupid as they seemed to be, those cruisers! They have made their escape by a simple operation, by hauling off all at the same time to their right on the tack away from the battleships. And the battleships have only one course open if they want the engagement to continue—they, too, must bear off to their right at the same instant and press on the chase. But it must be done at once or it will be too late . . .

Fargue, still perched on his seat, with his head in the armored sighting-hood, looks through the slits. Come now! That's not half bad! . . . the manœuver has been perfectly executed. Hardly had the signal flag been hoisted close up at the mainmast of the flag-ship than it was hauled down again, obeyed. Each ship is in its correct position. The "line ahead" has now become "line abreast," that is to say, the battleships are now forging ahead, side by side, with their bows pointing at the enemy, each one striving neither to pass or be passed by the next ship. . . . By no means an easy task to accomplish! But look! There is irregularity! The *Auersted,* the next ship on the port side, has lost nearly a length, and on the starboard side the *Eckmull* has gained a length and a half. Fargue demonstrates his opinion of them by spitting through the embrasure. Heavens! Is it only there, on board the *Fontenoy,* that sufficient care is taken to keep the signaled speed for five minutes together? Are they all asleep in those engine-rooms? Lord! What gems of engineers they have! It's a scandal. And Fargue spits again with emphasis. Behind him, Gourvès, Le Kellec, Fontan and several others are smiling in derision, taking their cue from their officer . . . A fine "line abreast," very fine!

But they are not there to amuse themselves. The working of the guns has slackened off, and Fargue turns round saying sharply:

"Well, Gourvès, do you mean to get loaded by

to-morrow, or do you think to-day will do as well?"

This sudden call to order runs through the crews, from Gourvès to Fontan, from Fontan to Brénéol, from Brénéol to Martin. And immediately the whole turret springs to its task. But again some one has groused under his breath. And again Fargue, anxious, wonders—how far is their discipline sound? How far can it be relied upon?

"Stand by . . . Same target. Bearing, ninety degrees! . . . Train right, third speed! . . . GOOD GOD!"

The order dies away in the mouth of the officer . . .

This is what has happened: the battleships have resumed their formation "line ahead" in order to double round and envelop the van of the opposing fleet, and to baffle this attempt, the cruisers have turned, and are steaming on a parallel course.

This accounts for the alteration in the aim, each ship having swung ninety degrees to the left. Only —something has gone wrong; either the rudder of the steering-gear or the tiller-chains, nobody knows for certain, there has been no time to find out yet, and the *Fontenoy*, instead of swinging round in time with the other ships, does not leave her course, and goes ahead in a straight line—in a straight line!— while the *Eckmull* on the starboard side swings, swings round perpendicularly on to the *Fontenoy*. Collision! Unavoidable collision! . . . Collision that means the burying of the *Eckmull's* ram in the *Fontenoy's* side, and instantly the *Fontenoy* will turn turtle and founder, just as the *Victoria* did in 1893 when rammed by the *Camperdown*. Death! Instant death rushing upon them! And nothing to be done! Nothing to be even attempted!

In spite of himself, Fargue shrinks back and turns his head, glancing round the turret with a tragic expression. Ho! The horror-filled eyes of the officer have met the strained eyes of his subordinates, the twelve men who have seen what he has seen, who understand as well as he does, who are waiting as he is, for death—twelve men who nevertheless stand at their positions motionless, silent, disciplined . . . Oh! the noble, the sublime machine! The blood rushes proudly through Fargue's heart. Let Death come! The turret is ready. With an epic gesture the lieutenant tears his cap from his head, and throws it on the ground to salute in advance the thirteen corpses who will soon be slumbering in death, each hero at his post. Then Fargue thrusts his head into the sighting-hood, and settles himself face to face with death, motionless, silent, disciplined . . .

Death comes on apace. The *Eckmull* is cleaving the seas with the speed of a locomotive. The colossal mass grows and grows and grows. Her stern cutting like a sword, throws off the water on either side with a sharp ripple as she approaches the side of the *Fontenoy*. How many seconds more? Thirty? Fifteen? Ten? . . . Her forecastle, crowded with men who have collected there gesticulating, rushes on them like an avalanche. . . . Fargue, his eyes hypnotized, does not even notice that the blue-and-white quartered flag is flying from the mizzen, a signal that the *Eckmull* is "going astern" with the whole force of her three engines: twenty thousand horse-power fighting in desperation to soften the terrible shock. Nor does Fargue realize that the deck beneath him is quivering with effort: the *Fontenoy* is steaming ahead with every ounce of steam available, trying desperately to pass, to clear the fatal ram. Six propellers are twisting and twirling under water for the common salvation.

Will it be possible to clear? . . . The whole hull of the *Fontenoy* is now vibrating. The *Fontenoy* means to elude death. She has got into her speed. She hurls herself through the waves, she races. And the *Eckmull,* checked by her engines, which are working as they never worked before, slackens, slackens. Will they clear?

They are clearing. Heavens! How close! . . . There is not twenty feet between the prow of the *Eckmull* and the stern of the *Fontenoy.* . . . But what matter twenty feet or twenty inches. . . . They have cleared! . . . They have passed.

Three drops of sweat stand out like pearls on Fargue's forehead. All the blood has fled from his cheeks. He lowers his head to look at his men. Not one has stirred; not one has uttered a sound.

And Fargue, his eyes on the receivers, begins coldly issuing his orders again:

"Train right, third speed. . . . Range, eight thousand four hundred. Deflection, sixteen thousandths . . ."

LÉON FRAPIÉ

XI

THE POCKETS

By Leon Frapie

THE two hundred pupils of the Infants' School being gathered together in the playground, Madame la Directrice orders an unexpected inspection of pockets.

The children are not allowed to carry on them any object that it would be dangerous to put in the mouth, which could hurt them when they fall, or with which they could hurt their companions. In other words, pockets must not contain anything but handkerchiefs and good marks.

The inspection of those of the little ones is soon over; most of them have no pockets, a rag that serves for handkerchief being stitched under their aprons. But the others, the big ones of four and five and six years old, are almost always at fault, and the teachers have to carry little baskets in which to place the confiscated objects.

What a harvest! The poorer, the more miserable the child, the stronger the instinct to pick up things. The pupils at the Platrier's Infants' School make a point of searching the dust-bins every morning as they go to school.

Soon the baskets are full of a surprising variety of rubbish: corks, fruit-stones, nails, bones, bits of zinc, of leather, of glass, of stone, of wood, fragments of pipes, of combs, of feeding-bottles, empty blacking-boxes, medicine bottles, etc.

The teachers are too used to this kind of discovery, and too busy, to waste time either in scolding or in asking for explanations. A speech from the Directrice reprimands all the offenders, warning them that accidents will continue to happen so long as they disobey orders.

To-day, however, three children are taken apart because of the following discoveries: twelve francs and fifty centimes in silver, wrapped in paper, in the pocket of Eulalie Blant; a little penny notebook, quite new, in the pocket of Louis Galtousse; a knife that opens and shuts in the pocket of Georges Mélie.

They are to be sent, one after another, into the room of Madame la Directrice, who will question them and act in accordance with circumstances.

   *   *   *   *   *   *   *

"Well, Eulalie, and where does this money come from?"

"Madame, it's the money for the rent; mother gives it to me to keep because if she didn't, she'd spend it. If I keep it the rent gets paid."

A silence. The Directrice soon decides there is nothing wrong here. Probably the mother drinks or has some other vice that leads her to spending all she earns, and though this child is only six years old, her pale, pinched face, pointed nose and sharp little chin give an impression that makes you believe her capable of dominating the will of a weak person . . .

"That's all right, my child; be careful your pocket doesn't come unsewn."

*   *   *   *   *   *   *

Enter Louis Galtousse.

"You stole this notebook from one of the counters outside the bazaar. No, it's no use denying it, my boy; here's the ticket with the name of the shop on it."

Ill-usage has made the face of Galtousse into a mask set in lines of defiance. He is developing a morbid impulse to steal, steals from moral distress, for no reason.

The Directrice knows it is no use threatening him with telling his parents or calling in a policeman; he is too hardened to misery to do otherwise than remain totally indifferent; a desire for revenge, not repentance, is all such a course would raise in him. Something must be done to try to rouse the better part in him.

The Directrice rings for the school attendant, to whom she gives a rapid glance that asks for collusion.

"Come in, Rose. This notebook has been stolen from the bazaar. You must take it back at once."

Rose assumes an air of fear.

"But suppose they believe it was I who stole it?"

"So much the worse for you."

"But if they put me in prison, Madame?"

"So much the worse for you."

Galtousse looks at Rose. He imagines Rose in prison; Rose whose kind hands are always ready to help; Rose, who listens to every one's troubles and never scolds. . . . Ah! no! even misery has its limit! His thin little body jerks, his nose contracts, his eyes wander, his chin moves up and down, and he begins to stammer.

"I'll never do it again, Madame . . . never . . . never. . . ."

"Very well, I forgive you this time, and I will arrange the matter myself. Go back to your class. And you, Rose, please send Georges Mélie to me."

*   *   *   *   *   *   *

Georges Mélie has a sad little face, sad and obstinate. The knife found in his pocket is an old, inoffensive one that might be used at meals for cutting up your bread and cheese.

"Where did you get this knife?"

"I asked an old woman to give it to me."

"And she gave it to you?"

"Yes."

"Long ago?"

"Oh, yes, a long time ago."

"Have you ever taken it out of your pocket in school?"

"Oh, no, Madame."

"Then why have you got it in your pocket?"

"To defend mother."

Madame la Directrice is taken with a sudden fit of coughing, and the child goes on without being questioned:

"I'm not going to let any one hurt mother. I'm not going to let mother go again to the hospital . . . and leave me all alone at home."

The cough of Madame la Directrice continues to

be bad, and she only catches odds and ends of the child's explanation.

. . . "When I was in bed in the dark cupboard . . . and I could hear . . . and she was calling 'Help!' . . . I had nothing to defend mother with. I'm not going to let any one hurt mother . . ."

He relapses into silence and waits, his eyes fixed steadily on her face.

The Directrice is perplexed. She knows too much about the circumstances that underlie the lives of these children of the very poor to have anything to say about the facts that have been stated; rules forbid her to allow the child to keep the knife, but she does not want to confiscate it—and all it means to him.

She raises her eyes with an air of distraction to the curtains of the window, and suddenly she exclaims:

"Good gracious me! I'm forgetting that Monsieur l'Inspecteur is coming this morning, and the books not ready for him! . . . What was that you were chattering about just now, little one? I've no time to talk to you now . . . no, no, not another word! Hold this for me . . ."

She gets up, opens some files, and places a pile of papers on the table, and as she pushes them about to get the things in order, the knife falls on the carpet without a sound.

She turns her back and makes a long search among more papers. When at last she returns to her desk, the knife is not on the floor.

"Still here!" she cries. "What are you waiting for? Can't you see I have no time to listen to you to-day? Monsieur l'Inspecteur will be here in a moment—run back quickly to your class . . ."

*   *   *   *   *   *   *

The gas-lamps are already flickering faintly in the November twilight when, at four o'clock, the children leave the Infants' School. Georges Mélie refuses to stop and play with them.

As he hurries quickly home, his sad little face pensive and affectionate, he looks like a good child who prefers to get back to show his mother his good marks. But it is not a piece of paper his fist clutches at the bottom of his pocket.

HUGUETTE GARNIER

XII

THE FIRST SHORT DRESS

By HUGUETTE GARNIER

"COME, come, my little Solange, do stand up straight! And don't keep your eyes on the floor like that; you worry me. Who could have imagined that being brought up in a convent would have made a young girl so stupid? Even suppose you do look at yourself in the glass, you won't be eternally damned for it, you know . . . No? . . . You won't? . . . All right . . . we'll do without your opinion!

"A little higher, the waist-line, Madeleine, there! . . . like that . . . no . . . still a little higher. . . . Cut the neck down heart-shape . . . The skirt to stand out a little at the hem. . . . No, not like that! Better tack it together on her; you're sure to get it right then.

"It's not because 'Mademoiselle' chooses to sulk that she need look like a packet. Her first ball! . . . The first time I can show her . . . Try to make her do me credit.

"Till now I've been obliged to keep her away from me . . . You understand? . . . I put her safely in a convent a long way from Paris. Now it's quite different. Monsieur de Breuil lost his mother, and we were able to be married. You didn't know

we had lived together before? . . . If I'd thought
that, I shouldn't have said anything about it! But
that's me, and I shall always be the same. I can't
help taking people into my confidence; must tell
everything.

"Blue ribbon? Rose ribbon? Both . . . I like
that Pompadour effect. It's young; it's fresh; it
looks festive. Yes, I like it very much: use the two.

"Why can't you give your opinion, Solange, instead of putting on that lonely-orphan expression of
yours? I don't understand that chit . . . not a
word to say for herself, and never any enthusiasm.
Talk of ingratitude—thanks to her I know all
about it!

"No, don't try to excuse her. It serves her right
if I do say it before her.

"It's not as if she had anything to complain about.
At that convent of the Ladies of the Rosary—it's
every bit as good as Les Oiseaux—she mixed with
all the best people in the town: the daughters of the
lawyers, the officers and the doctors. There were
even two titled young ladies in her class! I heard
one of the nuns calling out names a yard long: 'Syl-
vie de Langeac d'Arbois . . . Isabelle d'Arthys de
Grandclos' . . . and side by side by them was my
Solange. Ah! it wasn't an easy job to get her in
there. . . . But when you've got friends with influence . . . You might think she'd be grateful to me?
Yes, you may well turn your head away! . . .
You've made my heart ache many a time!

"When I used to go into the parlor you'd think
she was ashamed of me! Fortunately I only went
twice a year . . . And you may take it from me I

didn't go there with empty hands. If she's not
spoilt, it's not the fault of Bon Ami . . . It's true
he knew her when she was a tiny tot; four or five
years old, just before I sent her to the convent. I
can safely say I didn't start life in a big way—alone
at seventeen with a baby in my arms! . . . I tried
to get on the stage as a dancer. It wasn't all fun,
I assure you . . . It's very hard for a woman to
pull through by herself. . . . I don't know what
would have happened if Bon Ami hadn't come along
just then . . .

"What's the matter with you? . . . Do you feel
faint? . . . Why are you shrinking down like that?
Stand straight, at least while the pleats are being
arranged . . . Not so full as that, Madeleine . . .
She's very well made, the child; she takes after me.
The bust is remarkably well developed for sixteen.
Oh, look at her blushing! . . . Think of blushing
for that!

"Where had I got to? Oh, yes, to my visits.

"When I went in, she used to look quickly round
as if she was uneasy. Good heavens, I hope I did
show up against the other mothers! A lot of dow-
dies dressed anyhow, no figures, straight hair. In
those days my hair was straw-colored, a bright gold,
like sunshine. Do you remember that shade? . . .
It was all the fashion and it suited me. . . . Victorin
had just got the right tint. . . . I was very sorry
when he died! No one, I tell you, nobody else anywhere was able to make me look so fair. But when
I saw it was getting serious with Monsieur de Breuil,
I had my hair done darker, golden-brown.

"Golden or golden-brown, I always made a sen-

sation among the ladies of the Rosary. A picture
hat, a suspicion of rouge, and they seemed to be
stupefied. And Solange used to look at me in the
same way. She used to come in as if she was afraid,
all covered up in a long gray dress with a hood, and
a cross hanging round her neck on a black moiré
ribbon. That awful gray dress! . . . I shall never
be able to forget it . . . quite flat and very long
. . . so long that it covered the tops of her laced-up
shoes.

"She'd sit down, cross her hands, and hang her
head—just like she's lowering it now. Look at her!
I once asked the Mother Superior: 'Reverend
Mother, does my little girl ever look happy and
light-hearted?' The Mother Superior didn't answer,
she just stroked the child's hair softly. I admired
her beautiful hand, not manicured at all, but just like
a wax model—it's only nuns who have hands like
that—and her eyes looked like deep lakes in her
pale, calm face. I was very sorry for her for having
lost her beauty, and I didn't repeat my question.

"Tighter, the sleeve, and higher on the shoulder.
. . . A cloud of tulle? Little roses on the hem of
the frills? Try them, we'll see.

"They are dull places, those convents, deadly dull.
I adore my daughter, but when I had walked about
with her for an hour or two, she never opening her
mouth, in a great park where you see nobody but
children in gray dresses and nun hoods, I really
didn't know what to do. To be quiet like that takes
it out of me so. Every woman has her own nature,
hasn't she?

"I was glad when at last the chapel-bell began to

ring. I used to watch for it over the top of the oak trees. I saw it move as if it was balancing itself before flying up . . . then the chimes came out in notes like gold that seemed to fall on the old trees and the smooth lawns, on the statue of the Virgin, on the white pebbles—on my heart. In spite of myself I used to feel as if I were delivered from something very disagreeable. I used to say to myself: 'There! That's over for the next six months.' And I used to think about the train back, about my friends, about a pink satin bedspread . . . anything, no matter what! Stupid, wasn't it? But then I'm so home-loving! I'm never really happy except when I'm in my own place.

"When I got to the end of the path I used to turn round to wave good-by to her. She used to be standing like a statue behind the grille watching me go. No fear of her throwing a kiss after me! Not to be thought of . . .

"Oh, splendid, Madeleine! That drapery is something quite new! . . .

"But that didn't prevent me feeling very happy when Monsieur de Breuil told me I could go and bring her home. I thought that Solange would throw her arms round my neck, clap her hands, and that we'd go back together gossiping like two friends. Sixteen! At that age a girl ought to understand all sorts of things. What didn't I know when I was sixteen!

"Well not a bit of it! When I told her I'd come to take her away, she just stood and looked at me . . . I thought she was going to be ill. She clutched the stone seat with her two hands as if I was going

to drag her away by force, stammered, choked:
'She didn't want to leave the convent where she had
grown up . . . nor her friends . . . nor Sister
Michèle-des-Anges who loved her so much' . . . the
silly prattle of a little girl. I didn't pay any attention to it; I was certain that when that hideous gray
robe was taken off her, and her hair arranged in
curls, she'd quickly change her ideas. . . .

"But I reckoned without her character. How dis-
appointing children are! Impossible to get her interested in anything. She'll sit for hours together without opening her mouth, her mind miles away. My
husband thinks she is getting religious mania . . .
nice for me, isn't it?

"Do leave off twisting your handkerchief into rags
like that!

"You'll admit I haven't much luck with her. I'm
the only one among all my friends who has a speci-
men of this kind . . . The others have daughters
who look like pictures, pleasant, affectionate, ready
for anything; real little women who steal their mothers' silk stockings and go out with them to dances.
But this one looking like a mute at a funeral, she'll
end by spoiling all my fun.

"Look here, Madeleine, you're a very sensible
woman, you talk to her! Tell her what she owes to
her family, and that she might at least look in the
glass while she's being tried on, and say what her
own ideas about her dresses are.

"No . . . that won't do at all! . . . the skirt
is too long. She can afford to show her legs, she
can . . . make it shorter . . . still shorter, Madeleine. That's it. Leave it just below the knee.

"So that interests you, that detail, does it? At last you deign to raise your eyes and look. Yes, look at it, my Solange, it's your first short frock! Aren't you pleased with it? But what's wrong now? What's the matter with the silly child? . . . Crying? . . . *Crying?*"

GYP

XIII

FLIRTATION

By GYP

MADAME DE TREMBLE,
FOLLEUIL.

A Small Salon

MADAME DE TREMBLE (*seated in a low chair by the side of the fire, is thinking*). To-day I've had nothing but boring callers . . . the Dowager de la Balue, Madame de Rèche and Cécile de Valtanant . . . they were very gracious, but their remarks were all either bitter-sweet or pointed. . . . Monsieur d'Orange and Montespan . . . they're not more boring than the others, but they *will* flirt, and that exasperates me! . . . [FOLLEUIL *appears at the end of the room.*] Why, there's Folleuil! . . . (*aside*) They say that Folleuil is a "remarkable" man . . . I wonder if he, too, will flirt? We'll see. . . .

FOLLEUIL. You are alone! . . . that's strange . . . as a rule your salon is so crowded with admirers.

MADAME DE TREMBLE (*coquettishly*). Do you mind? . . .

FOLLEUIL (*aside*). What's this? . . . (*Aloud.*)

I mind . . . without minding. . . . [MADAME DE
TREMBLE *stretches her foot out towards the fire.*]
Yes, yes . . . your feet are lovely . . . that's un-
derstood . . .

MADAME DE TREMBLE (*shrugging her shoulders*). It's not to show them to you that I am warm-
ing them . . . it's because I am very cold . . .

FOLLEUIL. What madness to wear little stockings of nothing at all like those! . . . What are they
made of, your stockings? . . . tulle? . . .

MADAME DE TREMBLE. Silk . . .

FOLLEUIL. Ash-gray silk . . . certainly very
pretty, but it doesn't look very warm, ash-gray silk?
. . .

MADAME DE TREMBLE. Suppose they are ash-
gray or another color, I don't quite see . . .

FOLLEUIL. Have I said a stupid thing? . . .

MADAME DE TREMBLE. Do you count the stupid
things you say? . . .

FOLLEUIL. You are hard! . . . (*Looking criti-
cally at her.*) It's true . . . your feet must be
cold . . .

MADAME DE TREMBLE (*astonished*). How can
you see that? . . .

FOLLEUIL. By the end of your little nose, which
is beginning to grow red . . .

MADAME DE TREMBLE (*getting up and looking in
the mirror*). Yes, you're quite right! . . . Bah!
I don't care! . . . to-day I am not seeing any one
. . .

FOLLEUIL. Not seeing any one! . . . And me?
What about me? . . . You don't care whether I
admire you? . . .

MADAME DE TREMBLE. Not at all! . . .

FOLLEUIL (*aside*). I wonder if by any chance
she's sincere. . . . If so, I'm wasting my time! . . .
(*Aloud.*) Oh! . . . So you don't care about pleasing me? . . . well, that's not how I feel with regard
to you . . . very much the contrary! . . .

MADAME DE TREMBLE. You are very kind, and
I am very flattered! . . . Dear! dear! It looks as
if the rain had changed to hail! . . .

FOLLEUIL (*annoyed*). Don't try to change the
subject with your rain that changes to hail. . . .
You're going to try to stop my saying what I want
to, aren't you? . . .

MADAME DE TREMBLE (*feigning astonishment*).
Have you something to say to me? . . .

FOLLEUIL (*nervous*). Yes . . . and you know
it. . . . [*He rises, walks up and down the room
several times, and finally stops behind* MADAME DE
TREMBLE.] Are they your own, those delicious curls
that hang on your neck like a curly wig? . . .

MADAME DE TREMBLE. No . . .

FOLLEUIL. Yes, I'm certain they are! . . . If
they were artificial you'd say they weren't . . .

MADAME DE TREMBLE. What nonsense! . . .

FOLLEUIL. Naturally! . . . and then if they
weren't your own they would be better curled . . .
and of a more uniform shade . . . this hair is
striped like marble . . . only you could have strange
hair like that! . . . (*A pause.*) I say . . .

MADAME DE TREMBLE. What? . . .

FOLLEUIL. You must look a funny little person
when you wake in the morning . . . I am sure your
hair is like a mop, and that your ears are red? . . .

MADAME DE TREMBLE. Do you know you are taking a strange tone? . . .

FOLLEUIL. Oh! You're going to become as . . . proper as that? . . .

MADAME DE TREMBLE. No . . . but you have a habit of speaking very familiarly . . . and when a man speaks like that to a woman, it is she and not he that people blame . . .

FOLLEUIL. People! . . . they can't hear us at the present moment, your people! . . . and I'm the last to complain because they can't . . . what I said just now was not disagreeable . . . it is very pretty to have red ears . . .

MADAME DE TREMBLE (*resigned*). You are going back to that? . . .

FOLLEUIL. It is a sign of youth . . .

MADAME DE TREMBLE. You just hit it with your youth! . . . I am thirty to-day . . . or, to be quite exact, I shall be at six o'clock . . .

FOLLEUIL (*looking at his watch*). In thirty-five minutes! . . . What luck to find myself here! . . .

MADAME DE TREMBLE. You think I'm going to age suddenly as they do in fairy-tales? . . .

FOLLEUIL. No, that's not the reason . . . and you know as well as I do what I mean . . .

MADAME DE TREMBLE. I swear I have not the least idea what can give you happiness in the thought that in half-an-hour I shall be thirty . . .

FOLLEUIL. Good heavens! Don't you know that at that moment one always kisses the person with whom one happens to be . . . it's a recognized custom! . . .

MADAME DE TREMBLE (*laughing*). Really? . . . And you think that I'm going to kiss you? . . .

FOLLEUIL. If you prefer me to kiss you, I like that quite as well! . . .

MADAME DE TREMBLE (*stupefied*). Kiss me! . . . here! . . .

FOLLEUIL. Here or elsewhere, it's all the same to me! . . . Anyway, we're quite all right here! . . . no one can see us . . .

MADAME DE TREMBLE. That makes it worse! . . .

FOLLEUIL. What is certain is that I glue myself here. . . . [*He sits down.*] And that I don't move till the clock strikes . . .

MADAME DE TREMBLE. You are wandering in your mind! . . .

FOLLEUIL. Not in the very least. . . . It's always like that. . . . It's the custom. . . . Consult the learned men and you will see . . .

MADAME DE TREMBLE (*laughing*). Yes, that's it . . . I will first consult some learned men! . . .

FOLLEUIL (*piqued*). Why not say at once that you don't want to kiss me! . . .

MADAME DE TREMBLE. Most certainly I will say so! . . . You are becoming impossible . . .

FOLLEUIL. Impossible? . . . because I am trying to make you understand what is in my heart? . . .

MADAME DE TREMBLE. What did you say? . . . I believe, heaven pardon me, you spoke of a heart? . . .

FOLLEUIL. But . . .

MADAME DE TREMBLE. A heart? . . . You!

Come, come . . . would you like me to explain to you the little intrigue, not at all complicated, that is running in your mind? . . . You said to yourself: "Madame de Tremble has come back from the country much too soon. . . . She is almost the only person in Paris . . . it is probable that she is bored . . . she has been a widow for two years; she must be on the point . . . it is my opportunity, now or never, to propose myself as a candidate." . . . Come, come, isn't it so?

FOLLEUIL. Well, supposing it is? . . .

MADAME DE TREMBLE. Come, then, speak! I await your profession of faith! . . .

FOLLEUIL. You joke about the most serious things . . .

MADAME DE TREMBLE. You call that a serious thing? . . .

FOLLEUIL (*a little nervously*). Yes, indeed, there you have it! . . . I am one of those feeble-minded people who find love a serious thing . . .

MADAME DE TREMBLE (*with a candid look*). I beg your pardon? When was it a question of love? . . .

FOLLEUIL. Pretend not to understand if you like. . . . I have loved you for a long time, and I . . .

MADAME DE TREMBLE. Oh! no! . . . not that, I beg of you! . . . avoid at least the absurdity of telling me . . . me . . . that you love me! . . .

FOLLEUIL (*trying to justify himself*). Yes . . . I love you! . . . Yes! . . . yes! . . . yes! . . . do you hear me? . . .

MADAME DE TREMBLE (*ironically*). And since when? . . .

FOLLEUIL (*confused*). Since . . . since . . . how am I to know? . . . what a question to ask! . . .

MADAME DE TREMBLE. Embarrassing, isn't it? . . . Do tell me just how it began! . . . I should love to hear all about it . . .

FOLLEUIL. You are very unkind . . .

MADAME DE TREMBLE. Not at all! . . . but I can't help feeling amused! . . . Never before have you paid me any special attention . . . never once! . . . I have even been the recipient of your confidences, a very colorless part to play, you must agree, but which permitted me nevertheless, to see to what an extent you liked . . . change. . . . Between ourselves, it's the only thing you do like! . . . You never even deigned to notice me, and now, all of a sudden . . . without any warning . . . without any reason . . .

FOLLEUIL. How without any reason? . . .

MADAME DE TREMBLE. Without any good reason. . . . No, this is how it is . . . there is, or rather, there is going to be in your existence a . . . what shall I call it? . . . a vacancy . . .

FOLLEUIL (*protesting*). Oh! . . .

MADAME DE TREMBLE. Yes, a vacancy! . . . You looked round wondering vaguely who would be able to fill the threatened void . . . and just at that very moment you were passing my door . . .

FOLLEUIL (*uncomfortably*). Not at all . . . not at all . . .

MADAME DE TREMBLE (*continuing*). You said to yourself: "Why there's the little De Tremble! . . . and indeed, why not? . . . she's not bad-

looking . . . she's vivacious and good-hearted . . .
we belong to the same set . . . she's said to be possible . . . it will be a nice pastime, no trouble con-
nected with it, and it won't in any way change my
little habits! . . ." Then you thought a little . . .
oh, just a little . . . not long . . . and you decided
to go ahead . . .

FOLLEUIL (*somewhat embarrassed*). There's not
a word of truth in all that! . . . I love you because
you are adorable . . . you're not in the least like
other women! . . .

MADAME DE TREMBLE (*laughing*). I was expect-
ing that! . . . When a man tells a woman that she
is pretty, witty, anything in the gracious line, he
knows he never can count on anything like the effect
produced by that: "You're not in the least like other
women!" Please go on . . .

FOLLEUIL. Well, the truth is I didn't dare "go
ahead" as you call it . . . I was afraid of being
dismissed at the first word. . . . I felt sure you were
much more serious than you seemed to be . . .

MADAME DE TREMBLE. But that is extremely
flattering for me! . . . Do you mean to say you
admit that any woman could resist you? . . . you?
. . .

FOLLEUIL. Oh! don't laugh! . . . it really is a
compliment, for there are very few women from
whom one can fear that! . . . Come, let us talk
seriously . . .

MADAME DE TREMBLE (*making a little grimace*).
Oh! No!

FOLLEUIL. Yes! . . . Tell me . . . it is impossible that you can have arrived at your age . . .

MADAME DE TREMBLE (*laughing*). Thirty at six o'clock . . .

FOLLEUIL. Rest assured I'm not forgetting it! . . . It is, I say impossible that you have arrived at that age without ever longing for . . .

MADAME DE TREMBLE. I've done that . . . often . . . but . . .

FOLLEUIL (*deeply interested*). But? ? ?

MADAME DE TREMBLE. But not for you! Good heavens, no! . . . I find you charming, bright, sometimes amusing . . . not to-day . . . but you are what is called "An Adventure-Hunter," and you never forget it! You do not come up to my ideal . . . for however stupid it may seem to you, I also have my ideal . . .

FOLLEUIL. Ah! . . . And is it possible to know it, this ideal? . . .

MADAME DE TREMBLE. No . . . for it doesn't exist! . . .

FOLLEUIL (*pointedly*). Are you sure of that? . . .

MADAME DE TREMBLE. That question has every appearance of impertinence. . . . How can you be so small! . . .

FOLLEUIL (*with an air of deep melancholy*). When one is very unhappy! . . .

MADAME DE TREMBLE. Unhappy! . . . Now you're spoiling it all! . . . You want to persuade me that all this is serious? . . . But that's how it always is! . . . at a given moment, even an intelligent man behaves like . . . the others . . .

FOLLEUIL. Tell me, have you ever loved any one? . . .

MADAME DE TREMBLE (*without conviction*). Certainly . . . my husband . . .

FOLLEUIL (*incredulous*). Oh! That! . . . No, I mean since him . . .

MADAME DE TREMBLE. Anything else you'd like to ask? . . .

FOLLEUIL. Or before him? . . . a little romance, platonic and stupid . . . all girls have gone through that! . . .

MADAME DE TREMBLE. No, nothing! . . . not even a young cousin . . . or a "fatal" professor with long hair . . . not even a favorite dancing partner . . . my life is completely lacking in romantic incidents . . .

FOLLEUIL. And when you married . . . weren't you disappointed? . . . did marriage bring you what you hoped from it? . . .

MADAME DE TREMBLE. I hoped for nothing. . . . I was ignorant of everything! . . .

FOLLEUIL (*cynically*). Oh! of everything! . . .

MADAME DE TREMBLE (*emphasizing*). Of everything! . . .

FOLLEUIL. Well . . . you must have supposed . . .

MADAME DE TREMBLE. Nothing! . . . I was the prey of a vague apprehension, an unreasonable terror . . . that's all. . . . I had the same sensation one has at the theater, when one knows a shot is to be fired at the end of the piece, without knowing exactly with which weapon, and at what moment. . . . I wanted to stuff up my ears and ask to go away . . .

FOLLEUIL (*laughing*). Poor old Tremble! . . .

(*Serious.*) Tell me . . . at the present time they all make love to you all the time, don't they? . . .

MADAME DE TREMBLE. If any one asks you, you can say you know nothing about it. . . .

FOLLEUIL. I beg you to tell me . . . it makes me uneasy . . . (*Aside.*) the funny part of it is, it's true; it does worry me! Is it possible that I really am falling in love with her? . . . (*Aloud.*) That beast of a Saint Leu, I expect? . . . (*Insisting.*) It is he, isn't it? . . .

MADAME DE TREMBLE (*vexed*). He and the others! . . . think what a splendid catch I am . . . a widow who loses her fortune if she marries again! . . .

FOLLEUIL. It's true a man must have a certain confidence in himself if he offers himself in . . . exchange for the three hundred thousand francs a year left by that excellent Tremble. . . . but surely without marrying again one could . . .

MADAME DE TREMBLE. Go the pace? . . .

FOLLEUIL. Oh, why such an ugly expression? One need not "go the pace" as you say, to submit to the natural law and . . .

MADAME DE TREMBLE. And according to you, the natural law is to have lovers? . . .

FOLLEUIL. Yes, it's quite natural for a woman to have, not lovers, but a lover . . .

MADAME DE TREMBLE. On condition, of course, that this lover is yourself? . . .

FOLLEUIL. Of course! . . . I don't work for others . . . and besides, I repeat I adore you . . . (*Aside.*) My word, I begin to believe it's true . . . (*Aloud.*) Yes, I adore you! . . .

MADAME DE TREMBLE. Don't let's talk of that
. . .

FOLLEUIL. On the contrary, let us speak of nothing else; for I assure you, I did not come here for any other reason. . . . Yes, Madame, I am going to make you a formal declaration. . . . Oh, you shall not prevent my speaking! . . . You can't stop me. . . . I tell you I adore you . . . and for a long time, too . . . for six months at least! . . . At first it was sub-conscious . . .

MADAME DE TREMBLE (*laughing*). Ah, bah!
. . .

FOLLEUIL (*working himself up*). When I became aware of it, I tried not to think of you . . . it worried me to find myself loving any one as much as that . . .

MADAME DE TREMBLE (*mockingly*). It must have been a change for you? . . .

FOLLEUIL. You're right! . . . I gambled, I traveled. . . . I began to play the fool . . . it was hard, for I'd quite forgotten how to . . . I spent a lot of money, I fell ill; they made fun of me . . . and all that to come back more stupidly in love than ever! . . .

MADAME DE TREMBLE (*astonished*). How odd you are! . . .

FOLLEUIL. You call it odd? . . . I call it idiotic! . . . to give one's heart . . .

MADAME DE TREMBLE (*trying to joke*). Oh! his heart! . . .

FOLLEUIL. Yes, Madame, his heart! . . . and a very presentable, very well-preserved heart, I assure you . . . and to give it to a coquette . . .

MADAME DE TREMBLE. Oh! no. Not that! I am not a coquette . . .

FOLLEUIL (*raising his eyes to the ceiling*). Not a coquette? . . . You are a coquette to the marrow of your bones! . . .

MADAME DE TREMBLE. In any case, I believed I had never coquetted with you! . . .

FOLLEUIL (*vexed*). That is perfectly true! . . . (*Becoming tender again.*) Well, since you have nothing to fear from me, let yourself go, try to love me! . . . I ask for nothing else . . . I am not exacting . . . I love you so tenderly . . . and love is so good . . . you have never known what it is . . .

MADAME DE TREMBLE (*protesting*). How do you know that? . . .

FOLLEUIL. I knew Tremble. . . . Poor fellow . . . I wish him no harm . . . above all at present! . . . but I am very certain it was not he who . . . and always provided that . . . since he . . .

MADAME DE TREMBLE. That's right! Become impertinent again! . . . Monsieur de Tremble was . . .

FOLLEUIL. Charming! . . . handsome! . . . elegant! . . . an eagle! . . . it is understood! The absent always possess all the virtues . . . there's no way of verifying! . . .

MADAME DE TREMBLE. But really . . .

FOLLEUIL (*working himself up*). But nonsense! . . . Far better for a woman to have had several adventures than one husband . . . at least she's silent about them . . .

MADAME DE TREMBLE. Go on! . . . go on! . . . Talk nonsense again! . . .

FOLLEUIL (*almost convinced*). It makes me very unhappy to see that you are determined not to love me! . . . why won't you? . . .

MADAME DE TREMBLE. *Won't* isn't the word . . . *can't* would be more exact . . .

FOLLEUIL. What shall I do to try and please you. (*Supplicating.*) Tell me . . . tell me . . .

MADAME DE TREMBLE. One thing . . . only one . . . not to be like those who have already tried . . .

FOLLEUIL. Then I'm just like every one else? . . .

MADAME DE TREMBLE. I don't say that . . . you might very well turn any woman's head . . . (*a pause*) except mine . . .

FOLLEUIL. I am sure also that you do your best to stop yourself from falling in love . . . or from being loved . . . you are afraid of gossip; of the opinion of society . . .

MADAME DE TREMBLE (*quickly*). To that I say no! . . . I don't care at all for the opinion of society! . . . many people criticize me, but none of them know me . . .

FOLLEUIL. Then be good to me! . . . Let me adore you . . . think! . . . Would it not be good to have a true love which envelops without troubling you? . . . to have some one belong to you . . . at your orders . . . who only thinks of making life bright and easy for you? . . . have you never longed for that? . . . Can't you imagine how the hours fly by when two beings who love each other are together? . . . What . . . has no one ever said all that to you before? . . . [*He takes her hand.*]

You have never listened to those who have spoken to you of love? . . .

MADAME DE TREMBLE (*a little moved*). I might have listened if they had spoken like you . . .

FOLLEUIL (*radiant*). Do you really mean that?

MADAME DE TREMBLE. Above all, if they hadn't spoken at all. . . . [FOLLEUIL *starts.*] Yes . . . the love I dream of is not made up of exaggerations, nor even of words at all . . . it should consist of caresses, of silent embraces . . . above all, silent . . . always silent . . .

FOLLEUIL (*aside*). The devil! . . . rather difficult at the point we've got to . . .

MADAME DE TREMBLE (*dreamily*). I always swore I would not love any man who was not superior to myself . . . a remarkable man . . .

FOLLEUIL (*uneasy*). Ah!! . . .

MADAME DE TREMBLE. And it appears you are a remarkable man . . .

FOLLEUIL (*modest*). Oh! As for that . . .

MADAME DE TREMBLE (*looking kindly at him*). Prove to me that you are that man . . . and I am yours . . .

FOLLEUIL (*amazed*). Mine, you are mine? . . .

MADAME DE TREMBLE. Yes . . .

FOLLEUIL (*bewildered*). You? . . . You who just now said "no" with such unparalleled decision? . . .

MADAME DE TREMBLE. Ah! . . . A woman can change her mind! . . . (*Smiling.*) You are very eloquent, you know. . . . Come, let us continue the conversation . . . where did we leave off? . . .

FOLLEUIL (*losing his head*). But you are asking

an impossible thing! . . . How can any one talk to order like that? . . .

MADAME DE TREMBLE. But I'm not asking you to be brilliant . . . not at all . . . only be a little remarkable . . .

FOLLEUIL. It is paralyzing to be talked to like this . . .

MADAME DE TREMBLE. That's foolish of you! . . . A remarkable man should never be paralyzed. . . . You should leave that to ordinary people for whom it is a great resource in time of danger. . . . Come, talk to me of love . . . you may say anything you like . . .

FOLLEUIL (*completely nonplussed*). What! . . . It's when I am off my head with exaltation, when I can't collect my ideas, that you tell me to—it's enough to drive a man mad! . . . (*Aside.*) I believe I am going mad . . . I don't know exactly what I feel, but . . .

MADAME DE TREMBLE (*listening to the clock which is striking*). Six o'clock! . . .

FOLLEUIL (*repeats mechanically*). Six o'clock. . . . (*Remembering.*) Oh, yes! . . . [*He goes towards* MADAME DE TREMBLE *and kisses her respectfully.*] Six o'clock . . . you are thirty . . . (*Aside.*) And I . . . my head is empty and my legs are made of cotton-wool . . . it's horrible . . . (*To* MADAME DE TREMBLE.) You are laughing? . . .

MADAME DE TREMBLE. Yes . . . do you know what I'm thinking? . . .

FOLLEUIL. No . . . what? . . .

MADAME DE TREMBLE. I'm thinking that if I were to say the famous "I am yours" . . .

FOLLEUIL. Well? . . .

MADAME DE TREMBLE. Well, you would perhaps not be very eager to . . . (*Laughing.*) Oh, what a funny face you're making! . . . [FOLLEUIL *takes up his hat.*] When are you coming to see me again? . . .

FOLLEUIL (*violently*). Never! . . .

MADAME DE TREMBLE. Quite a nice ending! . . . Charming pastime, flirtation! . . .

ABEL HERMANT

XIV

THE WRIST-WATCH

By ABEL HERMANT

I THINK one of the best fellows I ever met—an
Englishman, and therefore the best possible—
was James D———. Our acquaintance lasted six
years, but it only came to an end with his life on the
tenth of July, 1919. During that comparatively
short space of time I saw James exactly seven times,
and you might almost count the words that passed
between us. We were on very familiar terms, laughing and joking together; yet we never seemed to
penetrate beneath the surface. I knew nothing of
his affairs, nor he of mine, and in reality we knew
nothing at all of one another. We certainly never
made avowals of friendship, unless this was implied
in thumps on the back and calling each other "old
boy." Nevertheless, I had the conviction that he
would have gone to his death for me, as I for him,
little suspecting that I should live to wonder whether
I had not indirectly had something to do with the
cause of his death.

The day of our first meeting was also a tenth of
July, the July of 1913. I had gone about mid-day
to the Royal Automobile Club, Pall Mall. The day
was hot and oppressive, and there were many bath-

ers in the swimming-bath in the basement of the
building. Although, in accordance with the elementary rules of good manners observed in England, no
one paid any attention to me, I wanted to do myself,
and perhaps my country, credit, and I had thoughts
of making a splash in more senses than one. Among
the spring-boards I selected one that seemed likely
to do justice to my powers. I examined it, measured
it, tried its pliability, and took a dive, which though
I say it myself, was perhaps worthy of their notice;
but when I rose, my hands still together above my
head, my arms stretched at full length, I could not
restrain a cry of vexation. I had thought of everything—except taking off my wrist-watch!

I swam as fast as I could to the landing-place
with one arm, the other lifted in the air; but the
mischief was already done; my watch had stopped.
When I got to the marble steps, I was greeted (for
the elementary rules above-mentioned are subject to
exceptions) with ironical condolence and the most
frantic merriment by some dozen young men who
had witnessed the dive and watched for my reappear-
ance. The English are a simple people; a trifle
amuses them; they even seem to prefer that it should
be a trifle. Some of them told me that they had
not observed my oversight until the moment when I
was planing down; others admitted, with candid cyn-
icism, that they had seen it in time, and could have
warned me of it, but that they refrained from doing
so, because they had such a curiosity to know from
actual experience how a wrist-watch would behave
when plunged into cold water. And they all asked in
chorus: "Has it stopped?" For they are passion-

ately fond of the theater, and it is the final scene that interests them.

I noticed James D—— because he was the most outspoken and the noisiest of the group. He was then twenty-two years of age, and what the English call, without false modesty, a splendid fellow. It was not so much his size and build that distinguished him from the others; it was his fine face; the eyes so frank, yet so roguish, a look so full of life's joy, its health and its beauty. No one could go near him without wishing to share the vitality that radiated from both body and mind.

I asked him to tell me his name, a favor I asked of no one else. I was well aware of the solecism I was committing, nor was he less so; but he appeared to be flattered by my request. He flushed perceptibly, slurred over his surname so that I could make little of it, and instead of his Christian name, gave me its diminutive, Jimmy. After which, as they kept pointing me out to all the members who came to bathe as "the man who dives with his watch on," as they kept asking me, "Is it going?" and as this kind of celebrity did not please me, I dressed hastily and took flight.

But next day, the weather still being hot, I returned at the same time, and again met Jimmy, who asked me the latest news of the watch, and would have gone on ragging me about it till doomsday if I had not been leaving on the fourteenth for Paris. We had become so friendly that I begged him to give me his card; I could not give him mine, not having one with me, but I told him that my address was to be found in *Who's Who*. So it is that lasting friendships are made. Ours lay dormant for a whole year. I returned to London in June, 1914, and lost no time in visiting the club. There I at once met Jimmy, who greeted me as if we had parted the day before; but instead of saying "How are you getting on?" he said, "Does it go well?"

I complained of his not having written to me. He replied with true English candor, charming in its bluntness:

"I couldn't write in French—I can't even speak it; you, on the other hand, speak English so badly that you would probably not have been able to read it."

As a proof that his memory had not failed him nor his feelings changed, he invited me, with some others of his acquaintance, to a dinner which he laughingly declared should take place annually, and be christened: "The Watch Dinner." I objected that I should be at Oxford on the date fixed.

"All right!" he said. "The dinner shall be at Oxford."

The dinner accordingly took place at Oxford at the Mitre Hotel. We were six. We dined in a simple way, and drank nothing but cider-cup, but Jimmy indulged himself a little, laughed and talked excitedly, and when he emerged into the High Street, he was quite drunk. He cried out all of a sudden:

"Where is Magdalen Tower? I can't see it. They have taken it away!"

And he burst into tears. I pointed out to him that the High Street bears sharply to the right, and that no one could see the tower from where we were. He declared that he could not sleep until he had

convinced himself that they had not stolen it; that
he must see it with his own eyes—that beautiful
tower with its eight turrets. We led him to the end
of the street, and then brought him back to the
hotel. The next day, on our return to London, we
heard of the assassination of Francis Ferdinand.
The war broke out. I heard nothing of Jimmy for
five years.

I had no doubt that he had been killed. I was
truly grieved, and when I returned to London for
the first time after those five years, in July, 1919,
I often thought of him with a heavy heart. I even
felt that I could not go to the club; but at last I
made up my mind to do so. I found there an entirely different set; many officers, and some of them
terribly maimed, which made a shocking impression
on me. What made their condition more touching
and pitiable was the way in which they bore their
afflictions. They did not appear to recognize or
acknowledge them. In spite of all they might think
or feel, they insisted on being "like everybody else."
I noticed particularly a young man whose left leg
had been amputated below the knee: I saw him go
stumping along leaning on the shoulder of a small
boy till he came to the edge of the swimming-bath
where he took a header and swam about almost as
if he had the use of his four limbs. When he came
out, I found that it was my Jimmy.

It seems an extraordinary thing to say, but delight
at meeting each other after so many years and such
miserable happenings was not our first emotion. Our
feelings trembled in the balance. I read clearly in
his eyes that he would have preferred not to see me;

that for some inscrutable reason he felt shame and humiliation at the change that had taken place in him. It was, however, with a semblance of his old gaiety that he asked:

"How's the watch?"

He reminded me that, as it happened, next day was the anniversary of our dinner, the "Watch Dinner" that was to have been an annual one, and we decided to go to Oxford together.

Next day we went to Oxford, only we were alone this time, and Jimmy did not get drunk. He wished to stay overnight, saying he particularly wished to go out on the Char. Not more than two minutes after we had left the landing-place, a sudden jerk of the punt, and by no means a violent one, pitched Jimmy into the river. He never rose, and I did not recover his body, his poor crippled body, until two hours afterwards.

How came he to be drowned; he who, forty-eight hours earlier, was swimming with apparent ease?

It is my conviction that in spite of his attempt to appear normal, he had lost his love of life, that his meeting with me had too vividly recalled the old days, and that his death was voluntary. For I cannot make myself believe that only my imagination is in play when I recall that he looked insistently at his wrist-watch just before the "accident," and that I heard him murmur:

"Will it stop?"

CHARLES-HENRY HIRSCH

XV

ISAAC LEVITSKI

By CHARLES-HENRY HIRSCH

THRICE, under brandished whip of Cossack or clenched fist of policeman, hands covering head to protect himself from their blows, had Isaac Levitski to clear out of the railway terminus at Warsaw. For a fourth time he made his appearance there, trusting in God, whose laws he obeyed, to instigate some passenger, touched by the sight of his wretchedness, to give him his bag to carry, and bestow a trifle in return.

With the utmost caution he slunk into a dim recess from which he looked out for a job, shrinking within himself, as if it were possible to actually diminish his physical proportions. He closed his eyes to shut out the fear of his surroundings. Under their lids he beheld the Temple of Jerusalem in its first blaze of gold, marble and porphyry, as it broke upon the astonished view of his forefathers in the days of Solomon, the just and glorious King. This recurring vision heartened him into forgetfulness of the spitting with which the police had defiled his beard.

Threading the times and spaces of earth, his imagination turned from that mysterious East which had grown gray since the dispersion of Israel dissipated its resplendence, to Paris, where Jacob, the eldest of his sons, was studying medicine.

Any one observing him then might have envied the happiness of the hapless creature and the placid smile that brightened his face. With a feverish impulse he fingered the five locks of hair that fell over his shoulders, and the two parts into which his beard was cloven. In this action the reality of the number seven cheered his soul; for it is that of the branches of the ritual candlestick, and brings prosperity; being the number favored by the Most High because, since the Creation, it denotes the return of the Sabbath.

"Jew, will nothing but killing you make you hook it?"

He rubbed his arm before turning his eyes upon a brutal Cossack who had struck it with his nagaika, and smiled, for he could find a ready answer:

"If you killed me I should be even less able to go where you would have me go."

The soldier had the purple, bloated face of a hardened drinker. His breath reeked with alcohol.

"Sheep-tick, you understand me!" he growled.

Levitski hardly moved. His knees stuck out beneath his long black coat, greenish with wear, patched in a hundred places and foul with stains, many of them stiffened and encrusted. He rucked it up along all its length with fingers nimble as the legs of a hunted insect until they stopped suddenly and tightened. For by this manœuver he had got at a leathern pouch which hung from his girdle. In an instant the folds had fallen back, and he was offering a copper coin to the Cossack with a slight and very humble motion of the hand.

"Filthy Jew!" muttered the man in uniform.

Not without threatening with his whip, in token of his authority as a representative of the Tsar, did he take himself off haughtily and sullenly, pocketing Isaac's peace-offering. And the latter fingered once more the seven wisps of hair to bring luck to his enterprises.

Luck favored them. No one interfered with him again before the arrival of the train. Carrying the portmanteau and wraps of a well-to-do passenger, Levitski praised the Almighty with all his heart for having decreed, in His providential wisdom, that this stranger should speak the dialect of the Jews of Warsaw volubly and boast before a porter of being a banker at Rome and a count by special grace of the Holy See.

"Blessed Virgin, what an age it is since I have been here!" he sighed.

As he looked up at him, Levitski nearly ran into the Cossack whose forbearance he had lately purchased. This drew down on him curses which did not in the least prevent him from imagining that some day Jacob, his first-born, would perhaps arrive in a saloon carriage, with filial and fraternal greetings worthy of a son of the tribe dedicated to priesthood.

"Rough on rats, the Cossacks, eh?" said the owner of the portmanteau and wraps.

Isaac only answered by raising his eyebrows because of a policeman who might have overheard him; and his meek look expressed the entire resignation of a soul submissive to the inflexible and avenging will of the Eternal.

"Put them there," ordered the financier.

Having deposited the articles in the Majestic Hotel omnibus, Levitski wiped his perspiring hands on his coat at the hips and, by a knowing smile that accompanied the hint of his panting breath, showed the confidence with which his apostate co-religionist had inspired him.

"How many children have you?"

"Twelve . . . as there will always be twelve tribes!"

"Well, I'll give you twelve roubles . . ."

On the mention of this unhoped-for sum, Isaac flushed with pleasure and with shame—with shame at a thought which he hesitated to put into words but which yet found expression:

"I have also my mother with me . . . She is paralyzed . . . With Hagar, my wife, that makes fifteen mouths to feed . . . fourteen, I should say, as Jacob . . . my eldest . . . is studying in France . . ."

"Well, take that then! . . ."

Having counted twenty roubles, he was about to put forth his thanks and blessings, but the omnibus bore away his benefactor. In the distance, that individual made signs of farewell to Levitski, who returned them with profound obeisances of his gaunt body.

"Be off, vanish, hog's dunghill!"

The Cossack would have lashed Isaac's back had not the Jew foreseen the barbarity, and, with a sidelong bound, measured the length of ground which must ever separate a subject of the Tsar from an agent of his imperial power. It was once again the

ruffian whom he had mollified with his modest gratu-
ity. He clasped his hand to feel there the identity
of the coins, and escaped, keeping to himself a shaft
of easily-conceived irony which might have cost him
dear, even though it had not penetrated the thick
skull of the giant.

At the age of forty, when one has never been
blessed with even the necessaries of life, and has
toiled bravely from infancy, a man does not feel
inclined to run much. Levitski soon had to walk.
He panted with fatigue, and his breath came with
difficulty. But from his whole soul, his jet-black
eyes, his fevered lips, his frail body, came the free
breath of thankfulness to the living God, The Almighty, for His goodness to him. He reckoned that
a tithe of these twenty roubles would give him two
for the Temple; that he would be able to spare two
for Jacob's requirements; that he could buy a woolen
scarf for his mother, and another, nearly as good, for
Hagar. He pondered over the remainder with intense satisfaction, invoking a divine blessing on the
generous stranger and on his heirs and assigns to the
third generation.

Aaron Rubinski, the shoemaker, hailed him from
the depths of his large stall, as from a grave, in
which he spent three quarters of each day:

"Hullo, Isaac, you seem very pleased with yourself!"

"That's because it's such lovely weather, Aaron."

"I am as true a Jew as you, Isaac. . . . You are
pleased . . . on any other account?"

"Maybe, maybe, Aaron. . . . Anyhow, it's not
because I'm forty years old . . ."

"Jacob your eldest . . . is he the occasion of this joyfulness?"

"I am blessed in all my progeny, Aaron," replied Isaac.

And distrusting any words, the best of which would have done little justice to his sense of gratitude to heaven, he took leave of the handicraftsman.

* * * * * * *

The house where he lodged was at hand. By day it was like a pigeon-house by reason of the babel of children's voices. At night when the little mouths were closed, it seemed a tragic and mysterious necropolis owing to the anxiety of their parents to let them enjoy in profound silence the dreams that enfranchised them.

The aged Rebecca, the paralyzed grandmother, who was moreover hard of hearing, felt the approach of her son. An indefinable look of sweetness came into her eyes as her daughter-in-law watched her. It was the latter who, on the look-out, first heard her husband's step on the stair. Simple-hearted, handsome yet in the fading charms of a mother of so many children, she clapped her hands, and her eyes deepened with a dutiful tenderness:

"Here's father!" she cried.

But the children had also heard. The whole eleven jumped up, leaving what they were about. They ranged themselves along the walls, the six sons on the right, the five daughters on the left, each group in an ordered file according to their ages, to await their father.

There were some with crisp black curls; there

were red-headed boys and girls. One only, a little
girl, was fair, the ashy-gray fairness of the Poles;
for a dark mystery enshrouds the problem of birth.
Generally speaking, their profiles were of the ovine
type, a result of the Hebrews being so long a shep-
herd people. The youngest ones fidgeted involuntarily, not yet understanding the majestic nature of
the ceremony. The youngest of all, who was called
Benjamin, gazed intently at a spider in a corner of
the ceiling above his pretty little head, ill-poised
upon the weary little shoulders of this precocious
philosopher—a spider in the center of her web
wherein her prey was entrapped. And he built up,
in view of that drama, the vague theories which he
could have wept at not being able to expound in
words.

"Benjamin!"

At the feeble call of his grandmother he lowered
his head, and his big, black, fawnlike eyes met the
worn-out eyes that sought his.

Isaac Levitski opened the door and paused on the
threshold; then he closed it very gently. Then,
taking off his cap, he went up to his mother and
knelt so that she could kiss him on the forehead
almost without moving. Then he kissed the forehead of his wife, Hagar, who had approached him
in the manner of a handmaid. Then, beginning with
the boys, he gave his hands to his children to kiss,
and he kissed them on the lips as his fatherly heart
enjoined him to do. He lifted Benjamin in his arms,
and as was his custom every night, folding him to
his breast in a kind of ecstasy, pronounced the name
of Jacob, his first-born. So, from the grandmother

half in her grave to the frail little Benjamin, there were fourteen to commend, from the depths of their fervent souls, to the Almighty who creates, destroys, regulates and convulses worlds, the fortunes of a young Jew who had gone from Poland to Paris to study medicine.

Now, dropping into lighter vein, Isaac told them of his good luck. Twenty roubles! Father has brought home twenty roubles! The little ones had gone back to their games or their lessons. The older girls placed fourteen wooden bowls on the bare table. Not one of them now remembered that there was a Tsar; that there were Cossacks and police. They submitted themselves wholly to the law as laid down and administered by the Head of the Family. Isaac Levitski felt pride in their reverence and in his position of authority. Neither blows, nor sarcasms, nor spittings, undergone because so many precious lives depended on his endurance of them, could subdue his exultation in belonging to the Chosen People before whom the Red Sea parted its waters and left dry land for their passage, to the race of Judith and of the Maccabees, those lions, and of Judas Maccabæus, that lion of lions.

There was sudden thunder, and Benjamin dropped the broken top with which he was playing, and put on his cap. His head covered that he might be worthy to speak with the Lord, he opened the window; for he knew that the Messiah would come with the rending of the clouds.

With an instinctive gesture, Isaac touched the five locks of hair and the two locks of beard. Until the storm was over he gazed at the blue trails of lightning furrowing the darkened void of space.

And sitting down to table, all these poor people, after prayer, regaled themselves on next to nothing.

EDMOND JALOUX

XVI

THE FUGITIVE

By Edmond Jaloux

FOR the last hour it had left off raining. There was a dripping from the leaves of the great trees; a mist, white, wet and saturating, rested heavily on the dull air. The gray morning saw the heights of Buttes-Chaumont deserted.

A couple strolled up a rising path. The man was a certain François Chedigny; one of the world's passers-by, one of its loungers; one of those who go from love to love; always sincere, but always quickly detached.

It was at Nice, at an hotel, that he had met Dora Cleghorn. Her mother, a wealthy American, had married a second time at New Orleans, and Dora was traveling alone through Europe, exploring the picture galleries and occasionally painting in the extreme school of impressionism.

To see Dora Cleghorn was not easily to forget her: slender, lithe, with the swing of a swallow; a touch of gold in her pale complexion, a hint of danger in the candid gray eyes; an air of distant dreaming.

Throughout their walk there had been much debate.

"It amounts to this," he said despondingly, "you will not believe in my love."

She prodded the moist sand with the point of her umbrella.

"I cannot believe or disbelieve," she replied. "Twenty men have sworn to me what you have sworn. Still, I must confess that you appear to be the sincerest of them all!"

"Then you will let yourself be persuaded into belief?"

"Ah, François, François, you go too fast! I must know what manner of man you are first. What do I know of you? You are like no one else. You please, you charm me—you may be sure of that or I should not meet you as I do! But I do not love you."

He took her arm with a masterful touch; she did not withdraw it.

"You must love me, Dora; you must love me because I do in truth love you, because my love is no light fancy, but has the somber strength, the enduring force of a great passion."

She interrupted him, for they had come to the park-entrance where a car was waiting.

"I am pressed for time now, François. You shall speak of all this to-morrow when you come to tea with me . . ."

Dora Cleghorn lived in the rue Jacob, in an old house which looked out on a garden full of great trees. On the lawn all overgrown with ivy, were fragments of statuary that showed, now here, now there, the appealing torso of a goddess, the bust of an emperor, a limb of a huntress, the back of an Apollo. Chedigny was shown into an apartment which might be taken for a sitting-room, a drawing-room or a study.

Dora, despising conventionalities, was seated, Turkish-fashion, on a low divan. She clapped her hands when her lover entered. She was in high spirits, and chattered volubly—a thousand absurdities. But he could not laugh: he was too much in love; he was suffering. He asked the same questions that he had put yesterday.

"I am going to spend a fortnight in London," she said. "I will think it all over. Perhaps my answer will be 'yes' when I return. I must take time for reflection. You upset my whole life, you terrible Frenchman! If I love you, if I marry you, what kind of man will you prove to be? I am horrified at the idea of a master."

He swore to her that he would never be that. Next day when he went to the station to see her off, he carried with him a great sheaf of iris. There were blooms of violet, somber velvet splendors, blooms of blue that radiated in streaks sharp as swords, blooms of black and white that smelt of incense and extinguished wax-lights. When she saw these flowers, Dora was touched, and it seemed as if there were tears in her eyes.

"You really are a delightful person," she said. The engine whistled; doors were slammed; passengers who were late ran along the platform; others who had taken their seats were already waving handkerchiefs.

"What will your answer be?" murmured Chedigny, raising himself on the footboard.

"I don't know! Hope . . ."

"You will write to me as soon as you get back?"

"Yes, I promise."

She held out her hand, a little white hand, slender and delicate as that of a child. He kissed it—a long, burning kiss. The train began to move slowly, then more rapidly. Chedigny could not understand the expression in those eyes with the hint of danger in their candor; in the face tinted with the touch of gold. His heart-strings tightened—for intuition told him that she would never return.

Nor was the instinct unjustified. The capricious American did not write. She had given him her address in London. His letters came back with "Not known" written across them.

Then François Chedigny suffered agonies; he suffered cruelly in his love, but still more cruelly in his pride. For a long time he clung to hope; but at last he realized that all was over.

He forgot, as most men do; and as most men do, he married. But the wound was never healed.

After the lapse of eight years he received a little note. Dora Cleghorn was in Paris, and asked him to come and see her. With a violent exclamation he swore he would never again set eyes on the woman who had so shamelessly fooled him. But the next day he presented himself at the old house in the rue Jacob.

Once more he saw the garden, all in leaf and flower, and the ruined statues, and once again he was in the boudoir with its silken Chinese hangings. On the table were the same dwarfed cedars; everywhere the Japanese vases in various shades of green displayed their graceful or grotesque forms; but there was dust over all—a certain atmosphere of neglect.

A figure raised itself from the divan: not the fascinating Dora Cleghorn, but her shadow. Pallid, all the gold gone from her skin, the hair streaked with white, and her voice was harsh, broken, irrecognizable.

"My old friend, how glad I am to see you!"

And she held out a hand so thin that the rings were loose upon it.

"Why did you leave me like that?" he said, before even seating himself.

"Because I loved you, François," she answered, sinking down again on the divan. "I can open my heart to you now: I loved you. That is why I was afraid. Never, never, have I been able to realize any dream of mine, and I preferred to keep my ideal of you, to live in thoughts of you at a distance. Perhaps you do not understand this . . . it is a sort of malady of the mind . . . I have always believed that love ought to burn like a magic fire in the heart, throwing a lasting glow of enchantment on the lovers, and my mother's experience and that of almost all my friends has taught me that it rarely is like that. I could not bring myself to imagine living everyday life with you, our companionship disturbed by the sordid details of housekeeping, our love breathed on and tarnished by the thousand little vulgarities and accidents of daily happenings. And so I went away . . . I loved some one else before I loved you, and wanted to marry him, but when the time came, I couldn't carry it through. I know now that I never really loved him, and I have never seen him

since. It is different with you, François. I have
wandered from country to country, but thoughts of
you have never left me; my heart has been full of
you, and your love embodied for me all the beauty
of life. And I have found a certain amount of real
happiness in remaining faithful to a love that has
never suffered disillusion . . . And you, what have
you been doing?"

He told her of his marriage.

She sighed.

"You are very fortunate to have been able to take
it like that. I am very glad. Idealists always have
the worst of it; are seldom really happy. . . . I
wanted to see you before I set out for Switzerland.
. . . Yes, I am going to Davos. A year ago in
London I had pneumonia; I never got over it, and it
developed into tuberculosis. I believe this will be
my last flight. But who knows? Perhaps I shall
live to love you for a long time yet . . . Look,
open that box . . ."

He obeyed, and saw a heap of dried flowers.

"It is the blooms of iris you gave me at the station. I have taken it with me everywhere. But to-
day I am going to give it back to you . . ."

*   *   *   *   *   *   *

When he said good-by to her for the last time,
he carried the box away under his arm as one carries
the coffin of an infant. He went back to his home.
He did not want his wife to see the poor withered
mass, and he could not throw it away. A garden
surrounded the house. He took a spade from the

tool-shed and dug a hole under a big tree, and there he placed the box. As he covered it with earth, he felt as if he were burying a dead body—the corpse of his love.

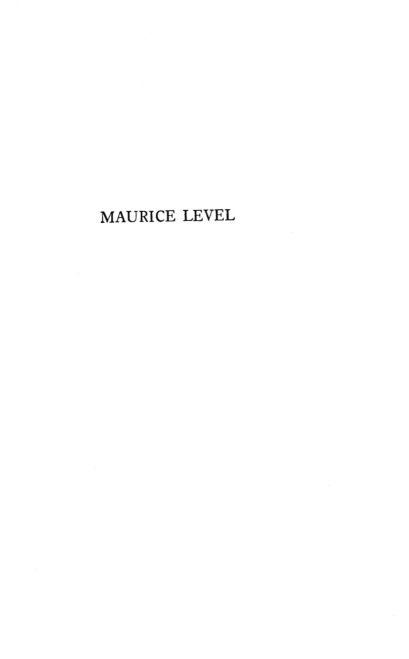

MAURICE LEVEL

XVII

THE DEBT-COLLECTOR

By MAURICE LEVEL

RAVENOT, debt-collector to the same bank for ten years, was a model employee. Never had there been the least cause to find fault with him. Never had the slightest error been detected in his books.

Living alone, carefully avoiding new acquaintances, keeping out of cafés and without love-affairs, he seemed happy, quite content with his lot. If it were sometimes said in his hearing: "It must be a temptation to handle such large sums!" he would quietly reply: "Why? Money that doesn't belong to you is not money."

In the locality in which he lived he was looked upon as a paragon, his advice sought after and taken.

On the evening of one collecting-day he did not return to his home. The idea of dishonesty never even suggested itself to those who knew him. Possibly a crime had been committed. The police traced his movements during the day. He had presented his bills punctually, and had collected his last sum near the Montrouge Gate about seven o'clock, when he had over two hundred thousand francs in his possession. Further than that all trace of him was lost. They scoured the waste ground that lies near the fortifications; the hovels that are found here and there in the military zone were ransacked: all with no result. As a matter of form they telegraphed in every direction, to every frontier station. But the directors of the bank, as well as the police, had little doubt that he had been laid in wait for, robbed, and thrown into the river. Basing their deductions on certain clues, they were able to state almost positively that the coup had been planned for some time by professional thieves.

Only one man in Paris shrugged his shoulders when he read about it in the papers: that man was Ravenot.

Just at the time when the keenest sleuth-hounds of the police were losing his scent, he had reached the Seine by the Boulevards Extérieurs. He had dressed himself under the arch of a bridge in some everyday clothes he had left there the night before, had put the two hundred thousand francs in his pocket, and, making a bundle of his uniform and satchel, he had weighted it with a large stone and dropped it into the river; then, unperturbed, he had returned to Paris. He slept at an hotel, and slept well. In a few hours he had become a consummate thief.

Profiting by his start, he might have taken a train across the frontier. He was too wise to suppose that a few hundred kilometers would put him beyond the reach of the gendarmes, and he had no illusions as to the fate that awaited him. He would most assuredly be arrested. Besides, his plan was a very different one.

When daylight came, he enclosed the two hundred

thousand francs in an envelope, sealed it with five seals, and went to a lawyer.

"Monsieur," said he, "this is why I have come to you. In this envelope I have some securities, papers that I want to leave in safety. I am going for a long journey, and I don't know when I shall return. I should like to leave this packet with you. I suppose you have no objection to my doing so?"

"None whatever. I'll give you a receipt."

He assented, then began to think. A receipt? Where could he put it? To whom entrust it? If he kept it on his person, he would certainly lose his deposit. He hesitated, not having foreseen this complication. Then he said easily:

"I am alone in the world, without relations and friends. The journey I intend making is not without danger. I should run the risk of losing the receipt, or it might be destroyed. Would it not be possible for you to take possession of the packet and place it in safety among your documents, and when I return, I should merely have to tell you, or your successor, my name?"

"But if I do that . . ."

"State on the receipt that it can only be claimed in this way. At any rate, if there is any risk, it is mine."

"Agreed! What is your name?"

He replied without hesitation:

"Duverger, Henri Duverger."

When he got back to the street, he breathed a sigh of relief. The first part of his program was over. They could clap the handcuffs on him now: the substance of his theft was beyond reach.

He had worked things out with cold deliberation on these lines: on the expiration of his sentence he would claim the deposit. No one would be able to dispute his right to it. Four or five unpleasant years to be gone through, and he would be a rich man! It was preferable to spending his life trudging from door to door collecting debts. He would go to live in the country. To every one he would be "Monsieur Duverger." He would grow old in peace and contentment, known as an honest, charitable man—for he would spend some of the money on others.

He waited twenty-four hours longer to make sure the numbers of the notes were not known, and reassured on this point, he gave himself up, a cigarette between his lips.

Another man in his place would have invented some story. He preferred to tell the truth, to admit the theft. Why waste time? But at his trial, as when he was first charged, it was impossible to drag from him a word about what he had done with the 200,000 francs. He confined himself to saying:

"I don't know. I fell asleep on a bench. . . . In my turn I was robbed."

Thanks to his irreproachable past he was condemned to only five years' penal servitude. He heard the sentence without moving a muscle. He was thirty-five. At forty, he would be free and rich. He considered the confinement a small, necessary sacrifice.

In the prison where he served his sentence he was a model for all the others, just as he had been a model employee. He watched the slow days pass without impatience or anxiety, concerned only about his health.

At last the day of his discharge came. They gave him back his little stock of personal effects, and he left with but one idea in his mind, that of getting to the lawyer. As he walked along, he imagined the coming scene.

He would arrive. He would be ushered into the impressive office. Would the lawyer recognize him? He would look in the glass: decidedly he had grown considerably older, and no doubt his face bore traces of his experience. No, certainly the lawyer would not recognize him. Ha! Ha! It would add to the humor of the situation.

"What can I do for you, Monsieur?"

"I have come for a deposit I made here five years ago."

"Which deposit? In what name?"

"In the name of Monsieur . . ."

Ravenot stopped, suddenly murmuring:

"How extraordinary. I can't remember the name I gave."

He racked his brains—a blank! He sat down on a bench, and feeling that he was growing unnerved, reasoned with himself.

"Come, come! Be calm! Monsieur . . . Monsieur . . . It began with . . . which letter?"

For an hour he sat lost in thought, straining his memory, groping after something that might suggest a clue. A waste of time. The name danced in front of him, round about him: he saw the letters jump, the syllables vanish. Every second he felt that he had it; that it was before his eyes, on his lips. No! At first this only worried him: then it became a sharp irritation that cut into him with a pain that was almost physical. Hot waves ran up and down his back. His muscles contracted: he found it impossible to sit still. His hands began to twitch. He bit his dry lips. He was divided between an impulse to weep and one to fight. But the more he focused his attention, the further the name seemed to recede. He struck the ground with his foot, rose, and said aloud:

"What's the good of worrying? It only makes things worse. If I leave off thinking about it, it will come of itself."

But an obsession cannot be shaken off in this way. In vain he turned his attention to the faces of the passers-by, stopped at the shop-windows, listened to the street noises: while he listened, unhearing, and looked, unseeing, the great question persisted:

"Monsieur? Monsieur?"

Night came. The streets were deserted. Worn out, he went to an hotel, asked for a room, and flung himself fully-dressed on the bed. For hours he went on racking his brain. At dawn he fell asleep. It was broad daylight when he awoke. He stretched himself luxuriously, his mind at ease; but in a flash the obsession gripped him again:

"Monsieur? Monsieur?"

A new sensation began to dominate his anguish of mind: fear. Fear that he might never remember the name, never. He got up, went out, walked for hours at random, hanging round the office of the lawyer. For the second time, night fell. He clutched his head in his hands and groaned:

"I shall go mad."

A terrible idea had now taken possession of his mind; he had 200,000 francs in notes, 200,000 francs, acquired by dishonesty, of course, but his, and they were out of his reach. To get them he had undergone five years in prison and now he could not touch them. The notes were there waiting for him, and one word, a mere word he could not remember, stood, an insuperable barrier, between him and them. He beat with clenched fists on his head, feeling his reason trembling in the balance; he stumbled against lamp-posts with the sway of a drunken man, tripped over curbstones. It was no longer an obsession or a torment. It had become a frenzy of his whole being, of his brain and of his flesh. He had now become convinced that he would never remember. His imagination conjured up a sardonic laugh that rang in his ears; people in the streets seemed to point at him as he passed. His steps quickened into a run that carried him straight ahead, knocking up against the passers-by, oblivious of the traffic. He wished to strike back, to be run over, crushed out of existence.

"Monsieur? Monsieur?"

At his feet the Seine flowed by, a muddy green spangled with the reflections of the bright stars. He sobbed out:

"Monsieur . . .? Oh, that name! That name!"

He went down the steps that led to the river, and lying face downwards, worked himself towards it to cool his face and hands. He was panting; the water drew him . . . drew his hot eyes . . . his ears . . . his whole body. He felt himself slipping, and unable to cling to the steep bank, he fell. The shock of the cold water set every nerve a-tingle. He struggled . . . thrust out his arms . . . flung his head up . . . went under . . . rose to the surface again, and with a sudden mighty effort, his eyes staring from his head, he yelled:

"I've got it! . . . Help! Duverger! Du . . ."

The quay was deserted. The water rippled against the pillars of the bridge: the echo of the somber arch repeated the name in the silence. . . . The river rose and fell lazily: lights danced on it, white and red. A wave a little stronger than the rest licked the bank near the mooring rings. . . . All was still . . .

ALFRED MACHARD

XVIII

BOUT-DE-BIBI . . . "MAJOR SIX STRIPES"

By Alfred Machard

IT was after he had found a policeman's battered
helmet in a dustbin that this extraordinary voca-
tion came to Bout-de-Bibi. Not that of holding up
the traffic from time to time, nor arresting dangerous thieves in suspect hotels, but he decided to be
Medical Inspector for the boys of the big apartment-
house in which he lived. In a moment of youthful
ambition he raised himself to the rank of "Major,"
and thanks to the generous gift of three pairs of
garters, " 'lastic color of the walls," belonging to
Trinité Thélémaque, to Marie Pigonneau, and to
Apollonie Trimouille, he had embellished his head-
piece with six wondrous stripes which assuredly enti-
tled him to the highest rank in the "Regiment of
Majors."

It was a simple game, played with due dignity.

He had called upon his inseparable companion,
Pancucule, to undertake the duties of the indispensable police sergeant, and had summoned Bébert, Lamoul, Biquot, Barbagna and all the others—there
were twelve of them—to strip before him and submit to an examination that was to be both thorough
and impartial.

Would you believe it? The proposition met with

the warmest welcome. Since the war, the "big ones"
never met in the streets without saying something
like:

"I'm to be examined on the 16th at . . ."

"And I on the 22nd at . . . at eight o'clock in
the morning."

The cafés and bars resounded with the wonderful
stories of those who had just come from the Medical
Boards, full of colds in their heads and the pride of
having rubbed shoulders with illustrious anatomies.

"Yes, old chap, I went in between a prince and
Sacha Guitry!"

Why shouldn't *they*, the conscripts of 1926, offer
themselves the virile illusion of going to the war?

With his father in the trenches, and his mother
at the workshop, Bout-de-Bibi was, during the afternoon, sole master of his parents' little flat. He decided that the privates should undress in the kitchen,
and then pass one by one before him in the sitting-
room.

*   *   *   *   *   *   *

Bout-de-Bibi had seated himself on the dresser,
and with a war-like air was drumming a military
march with his heels on the cupboard doors, making
the plates inside rattle. In his hand was a pair of
big field-glasses, proud spoil brought home on his
last leave by his father who had taken them from an
ober-leutnant.

Bout-de-Bibi thought that this scientific instrument
would help him to discover the defects in the young
conscripts about to appear before him, and explained:

"It's my microscope."

He tried it first on the police sergeant, and gave a cry of astonishment:

"Gox! What an eye you've got!"

The glass made everything look twelve times its real size.

The Police Sergeant Pancucule was not wearing those boots, those great boots, "caves of the winds," celebrated by poet-lovers of odoriferous delights, but he had put on his feet an old pair of hob-nailed ones which had been thrown aside as worn out in the bottom of a cupboard by Bout-de-Bibi's father.

"Sergeant, send in the first!" ordered the Major, focusing his glass on the kitchen door.

Pancucule opened the door, and bawled through in stentorian tones:

"First one, this way!"

Then, as Bébert appeared, dressed in nothing but the two tufts of rose-colored cotton-wool that protruded from his ears, he thrust his heel out sideways and brought his foot down heavily on the bare big toe. This was to give a realistic touch to the proceedings, for Cochard senior, who had stripped for inspection seventeen times since war began, declared on oath that the sergeant had secret orders to crush your toes. *Se non è vero . . .*

Major Six Stripes, silent and immovable, scrutinized Bébert through the glasses. The examination lasted a very long time. Embarrassed by the glare of those fiery, expanding eyes, Bébert suddenly became intimidated, and assumed the bashful pose of Venus Callypige.

But the voice of the Major, brusk and loud, ordered him to stand up straight.

The gendarme Pancucule, naïf and good-hearted, gave a reminder:

"The conscript is cold . . . his behind's all shaking."

Bébert was growing impatient:

"Am I going to be a soldier, or am I not going to be a soldier? Am I going . . ."

An exclamation from the major cut him short.

"Gox! . . . that one's covered with cress; it's growing all over him."

And straightway Bébert was rejected.

"Go and stand there in the corner while you wait," commanded the Major.

Crestfallen, Bébert did as he was told, and stood motionless, his nose pressed against the flowers of the wall-paper. "Another, Sergeant, bring another!" exulted Bibi in high glee. This time Lamoul, lank and lean, came in.

"Ha, ha! now for the Eiffel Tower," chaffed the sergeant irreverently.

The Major, still clasping his field-glasses, chortled with mirth:

"Ha! my lad, we must measure this one. . . . Get mother's tape-measure from the drawer in the sewing-machine . . . no hurry, Pancucule, I'm counting his cutlets."

But Pancucule had produced the tape.

"Lift up your arms," he said to Lamoul. "I've got to measure you . . . keep it still . . . 75 centimeters. . . . Put your head down, 35 centimeters

. . . stick out your leg, 90 centimeters . . . now for your foot, 30 centimeters . . ."

"It's not enough . . . rejected!"

Lamoul burst into tears. He hiccoughed, his shoulders heaving, inconsolable, touching in his despair:

"But it's not my fault! . . . It's not my fault!"

But the Major was adamant.

"I tell you you're rejected. . . . Go and stand beside Bébert!"

At that moment tragic cries came from the kitchen. The noise of a terrible struggle mingled with the crash of pots and pans on the tiled floor. There was a charge of cavalry in the copper, while a violent poker massacred some pots of jam.

The Major started violently.

"What's the matter?"

"It's Barbagna," answered some eager voices.

"What's he doing?"

"We can't stop him . . . he's struggling . . ."

"What for?"

" 'Cos the concierge keeps looking up, and he wants to put his back out of the window at her!"

To create a diversion and stop the accomplishment of this rash project, Bibi announced:

"It's Barbagna's turn!"

As the door opened, it revealed a topsy-turvy kitchen full of all kinds of débris. An urchin was rubbing his head under the tap. It was Biquot, and he was wailing:

"They've rubbed the soup into my hair; it's all sticking together."

Barbagna did not enter the room; he bounded. He was scarlet, foaming, wet with perspiration, like a young bull hunted from his dark lair into the sunny glare of the arena.

There was something about him that puzzled the Sergeant. He thought:

"He looks very funny without his clothes!"

And the Major, looking through his glass, was also astonished by the appearance of this new conscript.

"I say, Barbagna," he cried, "was your father a coal-man?"

This mysterious question puzzled Barbagna, and he calmed down.

"Why?"

" 'Cos . . . Well, you can see for yourself. . . . Get on the little table and look at yourself in the glass over the mantel-piece."

Unfortunate Barbagna! A few moments ago, in the course of the struggle in which the others had banded against him, he had fallen into the coal-box.

It was impossible to have a soldier of this color, and he was ignominiously rejected. The Major's harsh voice dismissed him.

Meanwhile, however, the Major himself seemed to be becoming highly nervous. His mocking eyes, generally full of laughter, had become somber, their gaze fixed ahead. He mumbled strange words in a threatening tone. At intervals, there were loud, long sighs, and something like a groan as he muttered:

"Pots of jam . . . the saucepan-handle . . . the soup . . . mother . . . hiding . . ."

Hastily and with rage he rejected all the other

conscripts, sent them into the dining-room, and ordered them to turn to the wall.   Then he disappeared quickly into the kitchen.

The unhappy twelve, dominated by his authoritative voice, waited, they hardly knew why, under the menace of the Sergeant's hob-nailed boots, the order to dress themselves.

And Biquot, his hair all clotted together, kept on wailing:

"I smell of leeks . . . it's no good . . . I smell of leeks . . . I shall always smell of leeks . . ."

Suddenly, a voice—such a voice of hate, a voice ringing with satisfied revenge, shouted from behind the carefully-bolted kitchen door.

"So you've broken me mother's kitchen to bits, have you? . . . All right; what I've done is, I've thrown your things out of the window, all your old shirts and your shoes, and your pants. . . . Out of the window!! Into the street! . . . Ha! Ha! And Biquot's flannel-waistcoat fell on top of a motor-bus!"

PIERRE MAC ORLAN

XIX

THE PHILANTHROPIST

By PIERRE MAC ORLAN

BEFORE settling down to live on his income in a house arranged according to his taste, M. de Tire-Moulure sought out in the first place a district where the inhabitants were poor enough to enable him to give a free rein to his constitutional benevolence.

On the coast of Brittany he found the Land of Promise that had filled his dreams, in the shape of a little god-forsaken town bordering on a heath about as fertile as the shell of a turtle.

The place was suitable in all respects. M. de Tire-Moulure took a comfortable house, and when his furniture had been moved into it, he began to make anxious inquiries concerning the distressful population of the neighborhood.

He could not help feeling the pleasurable thrill of a pig when its back is scratched on learning that cadgers and mumpers of every description, of every size, sex and age, infested the vicinity, giving this lost corner of the world the seductive appearance of being peopled by the crowd that frequents places where miraculous cures are expected.

The best traditions of the race of beggars were preserved in this Breton Thebaid as perfectly as pickles are in vinegar or flies in syrup. No inhuman notice to the effect that begging was prohibited interposed to stop the development of their curious industry. The master-beggars of bygone days, those who, with mouth spluttering foam as a result of chewing ground-ivy, imitated the convulsions of epilepsy, or those who manufactured hideous tumors by fastening to their legs a raw ox-spleen distended with blood and milk—such types of past greatness seemed to live again amid the appropriate surroundings of this abominable locality. M. de Tire-Moulure rubbed his hands; then put them in his pocket, and distributed *largesse* right and left to the extent of ten centimes or four sous.

When the worthy man went to the station to catch the train to Nantes, an occasional visit there being the only form of amusement the locality afforded, his gratification oozed from every pore as he found himself escorted by all the blind, crippled, deformed, cretinous, plague-stricken, one-armed, besotted, bone-lazy wrecks whom his philanthropy attracted to his breeches-pockets as valerian attracts cats.

Among these picturesque creatures, M. de Tire-Moulure had taken a special liking to a certain unfinished piece of humanity, whose screw-like construction suggested a dirty wet cloth that had been wrung out, but who was the only one who did not invoke God and the Saints, using instead something of a Parisian patter that was very agreeable to the smiling benefactor.

If Yahn, the blind man, hymned his miseries in the Breton of Quimper, if Yorick psalmed his distresses

in the dialect of Vannes, Bijou—that was the name
of M. de Tire-Moulure's protégé—Bijou brought
into this fraternity the personal note of his natural
tone and the up-to-date audacity of his ballads.

From ten to twelve, Bijou perambulated the High
Street arrayed in a deplorable sailor suit of canvas
that was once blue, but now was as spotted as the
patched dress of harlequin. His cap in his hand,
his legs crooked like those of a basset, he howled
before well-to-do houses the song for which he had
a particular affection, and which always proved pro-
ductive.

> With treacherous smile and words of guile
> He led astray the ga-a-mine,
> But left her dead on truckle bed,
> Devoured by fleas and fa-a-mine.

M. de Tire-Moulure never omitted to give two
sous to the artiste, who after a "Thank you, gents
and ladies!" renewed his vocal efforts under a sun
strong enough to melt the nails in boards.

As time went on, a friendship grew between the
man of leisure and the busy vocalist. Every day
Bijou came and held out his hand to M. de Tire-
Moulure, and the latter, feeling in his pocket, gave
him two sous.

This event was as certain in the life of the philanthropist as the arrival of the morning paper, announced at his door by the joyous blast of the horn
of Goazec, the newspaper-man.

As a rule, Bijou exercised his talents under the
balcony of the Café Mittonne on the market-place.

Always in the same position, his back against a lime-tree, he awaited complacently the arrival of his patron. The meeting always took place at the same hour with astronomical exactitude. Hand held out by Bijou, hand seeking pocket by gentleman.

This daily action became such a habit in the existence of these two beings that one morning M. de Tire-Moulure, finding himself at Bijou's tree, dropped two sous into space unconscious of the fact that the actual Bijou was not present.

It is thus with many habits; they seem innocent enough when first they are formed, but in the end they may have a fatal importance. And so it happened with M. de Tire-Moulure.

It chanced that on a certain day the good man went out to take a walk on the banks of a small, but somewhat deep stream. His mind elsewhere, his eyes unobservant, the philanthropist unconsciously adopted the locomotive method of the crab, and this had the effect of precipitating him into the water, not, however, without permitting him to describe a graceful parabola.

As soon as the protector of the poor found himself in the water, and could therefore have no doubt as to the nature of his misfortune, he began to raise cries even more piercing than those of enthusiasm, doubtless with the intention of letting some charitable soul know of his misfortune.

The charitable soul appeared in the person of Bijou, who, seeing the sad plight of his patron, hastened to his assistance, hoping by saving his life to discharge the debt of all the ten-centime pieces he had received. Happy, in short, to get quit of his many obligations at so cheap a rate, he ran to the bank, stooped down and, with the old instinctive gesture, held out his hand to M. de Tire-Moulure.

That gesture caused the death of the philanthropist. Before that extended hand, broad as a tennis-racquet, which appeared to be offering itself in the habitual manner, instinctively he put his hand in his pocket and placed two sous in the animated begging-bowl presented by Bijou.

It was his last effort. Exhausted, and already three-quarters full of water, M. de Tire-Moulure went down to explore the bottom of the river, leaving to other philanthropists, equipped with poles and grappling-irons, the delicate business of getting him out after a search of twenty-four hours.

BINET-VALMER

XX

WHEN SHE WAS DEAD . . .

By BINET-VALMER

A T the moment when she turned to her mirror
with the look of a woman who, her toilette
finished, composes her face into the expression with
which she meets her friends, as she drew round her
shoulders and bosom the rich chinchilla of her evening cloak, she grew pale, her eyes opened to their
widest extent as if they had suddenly become aware
of their own mystery—of that mystery that attracted
us all. The lips grew livid; the smile, the beautiful
smile that was both humorous and tired, changed to
a tragic contortion, and her face—I saw it an hour
later—became like that of the mutilated statue in
the Museum at Athens, the head of a Goddess Con-
templating Death.

Without uttering a sound, Madame de Vrénel
fell full length on the white bear-skin rug before her
dressing-table. At the noise of the fall, Thérèse,
the maid, ran in. Madame de Vrénel was dead. A
little blood was coming from her mouth, and a great
tear ran down from the corner of an eyelid.

A splendid death! Fernande de Vrénel had never
been in more perfect health than this year. Occasionally a feeling of oppression, and a hand raised
quickly to the breast. The aneurism had developed

slowly, without pain. If Nature considered us in any way, she would always act like this.

Instantly the house became full of the terrified clamor of the servants, and Maurice de Longy, who was waiting in the hall, his hat on his head, his scarf round his neck, rushed upstairs. The parquet floor resounded as he dropped heavily on his knees by the side of the dead woman. The doctor had been sent for, and while they waited, Maurice lifted Fernande in his arms and placed her on the bed. The tear had left its trace on the powdered cheek, and the blood was trickling down by the side of the finely-modeled chin. Pushed forward by the pillow, the pale gold waving hair framed the face. You could hear the silence.

At the head of the bed, Maurice, a man whose features had been hardened into impassivity by a political career, bent over the quiet form with his face distraught, and the maid, Thérèse, who usually looked the soubrette of comedy, had the air of a peasant as she crossed herself.

The doctor hurried in. At once precision routed disorder. Then came the words:

"There is nothing to be done."

The sobs that broke out were dominated by the voice at the telephone summoning relatives.

Their emotion created an atmosphere of fever, the excitement that helps us through tragedies. Every one treated Maurice de Longy as the master of the house, as if death had suddenly made official the love-affair on which Paris had smiled for nearly ten years.

The harmony of the relationship of this couple

had been welcomed by society. People respected it because of its double fidelity. Since the death of Monsieur de Vrénel, since the disappearance of Madame de Longy, who had gone away with a lover, there was hardly a day when Fernande and Maurice had not dined together. This evening they were being waited for at an Embassy. On the bed Madame de Vrénel lay in full evening dress. It was necessary to undress her at once, and the room was emptied.

Down in the hall, Maurice said good-by to every one, and by degrees the big house grew quiet again. It was in the Avenue du Bois, and it was winter.

Not a sound. Sometimes a servant crept by as Maurice walked up and down the hall. He had suddenly taken on his age. An hour before one would have imagined he was barely forty. Now he looked fifty-two, and his shoulders were bent as if he were old. The movement and rhythm of his steps helped to give form to his thoughts, which had been circling confusedly round the vision of a tear running down a cheek and a chin stained with blood, and the questions, puerile and selfish: "Why?" and "What will become of me?"

Once he had said to Fernande:

"How glad I am that I am so much older than you. I have come through several catastrophes, but to lose you would kill me."

And he was conscious of surprise that he was still alive, to hear his own steps, to feel that his heart was still beating in a body that seemed strong and robust.

*　　*　　*　　*　　*　　*　　*

The death-chamber was now in order.

To-morrow the priests and the prayers. To-night Fernande belonged to him. It was their last tête-à-tête, their last lovers' meeting—and as chaste as all the others.

Yes, the beautiful body whose outlines showed through the white covering had never belonged to this lover, passionate though he was, and those whom every one believed to be lover and mistress had only been friends.

He approached the bed. They had wiped the blood from the mouth. One day, long ago, before Fernande's widowhood, Maurice had kissed this mouth. Only once. Why? He had at the time felt sure that he would eventually possess her. She seemed to offer herself . . . But the kiss had been followed by: "Never again! You must not! You must not! We must never be more to each other than we are now!" and the woman who had coquetted with him had suddenly become a sort of saint. He had accepted the position. He had done all in his power to maintain it, even finding a kind of pleasure in the suffering it entailed. The most foolhardy of games, and one that intoxicates more surely than opium or morphia. An unhappy and incomplete love dominates the heart, and creates a lack of mental equilibrium. Sensuality becomes separated from love, and the love becomes a kind of malady of the mind. Oh, to be lying there lifeless beside her, free from the new torture of wondering whether he had been right or wrong! . . .

Again Maurice began to pace heavily up and down the room. Longer than its breadth, it had three curtain-covered windows. The bed was at the end of the room, and between it and one of the windows there was a portière that covered a little door that communicated with the servants' staircase, made there by the caprice of an actress who once owned the house.

They had often laughed about the door.

"Would you like me to give you the key?" Fernande had once said.

Maurice's face had changed color at the suggestion. Their relationship was pure enough for Fernande to be able to regret her own lack of temperament. "Something is wanting in me," she had said. And Maurice had replied by praising the beauty and nobility of purely spiritual love. Fernande had responded by her charming, weary smile. And now he was wondering whether he had been right in accepting the unnatural position.

Immersed in sad, strange thoughts, he continued to pace up and down. Time was passing, and the corpse had taken on the beauty that comes some hours after death. Fernande was lovelier than in life; she looked younger, and as he paused to look at her, Maurice realized how unique she had been, how incomparable.

He sank into the armchair by the bedside, weeping, his hands pressed to his eyes.

Suddenly an unusual sound, a crunching, a grating, filled him with the terror of the supernatural, and as the clock struck one, the hanging over the secret door moved. There was no light in the room but that of the candles at the head of the bed, and as he sensed rather than saw that the portière was drawn aside,

Maurice de Longy cowered in his chair. Some one came in on tiptoe, a man in an elegant overcoat, a man who was evidently not here for the first time, who knew the room well, and he murmured:

"Fernande!"

Maurice knew the voice. He started up:

"What are you doing here?"

And he who had stolen in like a thief, Philippe Dormeaux, a Don Juan with a reputation for great success in light love, started, and stood still. He began to stammer.

"Be quiet!" said Maurice. "Don't you know? She is dead.

The eyes of both men turned to the dead woman, who seemed to be smiling at them.

"Dead!" murmured Philippe.

"Yes. Go away."

But Philippe repeated:

"Dead!"

"Yes," said Maurice, advancing threateningly towards him. "Clear out!"

Were they going to fly at each other's throats? . . .

Philippe turned away, but the other placed his hand heavily on his shoulder.

"Stay! . . . How long have you . . . go on! Tell me! I want to know! . . . Oh, yes, yes, you shall tell me!"

He seized him by the throat, and Philippe, a coward before physical strength, confessed, hiding his fear under an ignoble vanity. The secret liaison which had given him this key and the right to enter by the servants' staircase, began before the death of Monsieur de Vrénel. The woman, whose dead face seemed to smile at them, had belonged to both of them at the same time without letting one infringe on the rights of the other, except on that one occasion when Maurice had been allowed to kiss her.

"You need not be jealous," sneered Philippe. "It was you she loved."

And he explained that for him she was merely a courtesan who succumbed to her instincts, the victim of her appetites, but with Maurice it was different . . .

"You have nothing to be jealous about!"

Maurice let go, and turned away murmuring:

"She never loved me. You don't know . . ."

"It is I she never loved," replied Philippe. "She gave me her nights on condition that I never saw her during the day. I was merely a servant who . . ."

"She made a fool of me," protested Maurice. "She wished me to adore her as one would a saint!"

"She wanted to be taken possession of as if she were a light woman," said Philippe.

Then full of his unclean experiences, he added:

"Most women are the same . . ."

"Silence!" cried Maurice.

In the stillness that followed, the two men gave themselves up to their own thoughts, the one evoking the chaste poem he had lived, the other the poem of the passionate flesh he had enjoyed. And though they remained there till dawn, till the odor of death had begun to be evident in the room, neither of them succeeded in uniting in imagination the two personalities that had lived in the quiet form on the bed.

PAUL AND VICTOR MARGUERITTE

XXI

POUM AND THE ZOUAVE

By PAUL AND VICTOR MARGUERITTE

ONE day when his parents had left him at home
as a punishment, Poum was exceedingly bored.
He had exhausted all the expedients of his fertile
little brain; he had worried the dog, had pumped his
shoes full of water, had taken fright at a cockroach,
had hunted the flies, had turned on the watertaps in
the basin, had yelled to his heart's desire, then had
called down dire penalties on the head of his friend
Zette because she did not come to him, had sniffed
vigorously to catch the smell of her pomaded hair
on the breeze, had dreamt that he was the Pope, had
decided to become a soldier and cut off the heads of
his enemies, had set his heart on a musical box as
a New Year's present, had invented a new and belit-
tling name for his tutor, had gone over the next
day's lesson, "the principal rivers of France are . . .
are . . ." without being able to name a single one
of them, whereupon a precocious hatred of the whole
world had fallen upon him, and emulating the ex-
tremes of a Nero who had read Schopenhauer, the
afore-mentioned Poum began first to hop along the
garden-walks on one foot, tearing the leaves from
the bushes as he passed, then he turned himself into
a locomotive: "Phou! Phou! Phou!" This brought

him as far as the dining-room where there was fruit to be pilfered, when—wonder upon wonders!—a rare being, whose oddity would haunt him to the end of his days, appeared before him.

It was a Zouave.

Perched on a ladder, showing baggy red trousers under a canvas smock, this Zouave was painting the woodwork of the ceiling. He did not seem in the least surprised to see a locomotive puff its way into a dining-room, and called out:

"Puffer's Town! Ten minutes' stop! For refreshments!"

As Poum came to a standstill, divided in his mind between delight and the doubt if he ought to take "Puffer's Town" as a joke or an insult, the Zouave looked down on him with a cunning air, showing teeth stained like a tobacco-pipe, then solemnly bringing the paint-brush up to the level of his eyes, said:

"Greeting, my Colonel!"

Poum assumed a haughty look, that with which he imagined his father, the real Colonel, half-raised his forearm when he returned the salutes of his orderlies. He even deigned to say condescendingly:

"If your ladder isn't firm, you'll have a jolly tumble."

"That would cure me nicely of my twisty-me-grims!" said the Zouave, who thereupon began to stretch and contract his neck in an odd fashion, and then to roll it round and round on his shoulders as if he wanted to throw his head out of the window.

A cry of terror and admiration forced itself from Poum.

"Oh! Bother!" The Zouave appeared very annoyed as he said this. "There's my eye just dropped out! You might have a look round for it, please, there, under the ladder, to the left."

And in truth his left eye was now closed, and it looked as if there was nothing under the eyelid.

"That's the second time it's happened from my wagging my head too hard! The last time was when I was out shooting with my friend Barbary in Tartary, and a crocodile gobbled it up that time!"

"I can't find any eye on the floor," said Poum, who was looking, half believing, so strongly had the Zouave's composure impressed him.

The man cut a wild caper, and scrambled down the ladder to the floor, snatching wildly in his funny zigzag descent at some invisible object which he apparently found and placed in his eye-socket, securing its position with a resounding smack.

" 'Ello, Matthew, old chap, how do you like being back again?"

He lifted his eyelid, showing that both his eyes were in place.

Much relieved, Poum began to laugh. So did the Zouave.

"Exactly like the crocodile," he said. "He laughed so much after having swallowed my eye, that out it came again, just like it used to happen when my grandmother used to swallow the five-franc pieces."

Poum's eyes opened wide in astonishment.

"You don't believe me, then?" said the Zouave. "Perhaps you never heard of my grandmother, Whiska Scaramoustacha, of Gallow's Lane, Burglar's Town?   For all that, she's very well known."

Very firmly, but quite politely, Poum declared that he had never heard of her.

"Have you a five-franc piece?"

Poum shook his head.

"Well, a two-franc piece?"

"No."

"You must have at least half-a-franc!" said this man with such commanding irony that Poum, though already feeling uneasy, wormed a brand new half-franc from the depths of his pocket where it lay between a top and a leaden soldier.

"There's no cleverness in this, a child could swallow it easy.   Never mind!   Ouap!"

As he made this barking noise, the Zouave gulped down the coin.

"Oh!   Give it back to me!" Poum begged.

The man opened his eyes wide.

"But how can I when I've swallowed it?"

"Oh!   Give me back my money!"

"Look here!   I must be getting on with my work. Painting don't exactly do itself, and what would your papa say?"

He pretended to climb the ladder.

"My half-franc!" groaned Poum.

The Zouave assumed an air of suspicion, and with an inquisitorial voice asked:

"Are you sure it was silver?   It wasn't lead?"

"It was half-a-franc in silver and quite new."

"But are you abso-bloomin-lutely sure about it?"

He put such anguish into the tone of his question that Poum stammered out:

"Why?"

"Because if your coin's bad, you'd better tell me straight off. I'm a dead man."

He gripped his stomach with both his hands, and his features worked convulsively:

"It was a bad coin. I'm poisoned!"

He began to writhe.

"There's only one way to cure me. Don't make any noise, and don't call any one. A nice cigar would save my life or a pipeful of tobacco! Is there any baccy here? Oh! How it hurts me! Half a mo' . . . I've heard say that a glass of rum is a cure. . . . Oh! My eye! What tortures! . . . or any sort of drink. . . . Ah! . . . Ah! Ah! la, la!"

Poum rushed over to the sideboard, snatched the decanter, and filling a wineglass to the brim, handed it to the Zouave, who was showing the whites of his eyes.

"Oh! Oh! Thank you!" He took a sip. "Why it's . . . ouye! Ah! the beastly stuff, ain't it strong! It's"—he smacked his lips—"it's A1. . . . cut 'em in bits and put 'em together again!"

He poured the rest of it down his throat and said:

"There's no more danger . . . the coin's melted!"

He looked at Poum with a frank, unanswerable look.

"Melted! Psst! Dissolved! Evaporated!"

"My money!" Poum began again.

The Zouave opened on him in a soothing professorial voice:

"There was once a queen who was called Cleopaster, in the time of Saint Anthony. One day she took and swallowed her ear-rings, and they were pearl ones, just because she took a fancy to 'em. Then she went and swallowed a great pot of vinegar to help digest them, and if she hadn't, Great Barbery Apes and Monkeys! they'd just have laid on her stomach.''

Then he added thoughtfully:

"There's no doubt about that. Look here . . . I . . . I'm a freemason. Ever seen the mark?"

He pulled up his sleeve: on his hairy white arm was a heart, tattooed in blue and transfixed by an arrow.

"That means that if a freemason tells you a secret, and you give it away you can be dead sure that a ghost will come along and pierce your heart, and you'll die. Supposing you tell your papa that you were talking to me, and tell him all that passed between us"—the Zouave looked steadily at Poum in a terrifying manner—"well, that night, when everybody's asleep, a hand will come crawling out from under your bed, and a big Death's Head will come squirming up and . . ."

The Zouave stopped short, for all the world as if the apparition had appeared and turned him into stone, whilst an awe-inspiring voice, issuing from a mouth bristling with a white mustache, sounded from the end of the room:

"Go on, Zouave, go on!"

Poum jumped like a fish out of water as he recognized his father, the Colonel, who said sternly, without even looking at Poum:

"Give back that little fool's money!"

The Zouave turned red, redder than his trousers, and returned the half-franc. Poum took it, delighted to have it, but humiliated at being described to his mystifier as a "little fool."

The Colonel looked at the sideboard, the unstoppered decanter, the empty glass. There was a dead silence whilst he chewed the ends of his mustache:

"Did you find my brandy good?" he asked at last in a sarcastic and terrifying voice.

Silence on the part of the Zouave, his hands held close to the seams of his trousers.

"Did you find my brandy good?" he repeated still louder.

Then lower than a whisper, almost inaudible, the voice of the Zouave came back.

"Yes, my Colonel."

"Delighted to hear it! Well, my man, I hope it's put some energy into you! Don't deprive yourself of the pleasure of going on with your work because I happen to be here!"

The Zouave leapt up his ladder and began to dab wildly at the cornice, transfixed by the lynx-eye of his Commanding Officer, whilst Poum, feeling very small indeed, tried not to sniffle as he turned his half-franc about in his pocket.

VICTOR MARGUERITTE

XXII

THE WHIPPER-SNAPPER

By Victor Margueritte

"EVEN an old soldier like me, who, in the course of his life, has been through some pretty rough experiences, finds himself not infrequently in situations so difficult that, die-hard and patriot as he may be, he is moved to the point of asking himself whether one really has the right to do what one does, and whether under the pretext that discipline requires it, he is truly justified in stifling in himself every human feeling.

"Of course I am not talking of the moment of actual fighting. At such times there is no chance to reflect, besides which you feel that you are fulfilling a lofty duty. You are driven on by the unarmed mass which, behind you, by every home-fire of your native land, is sobbing and waiting expectantly: you are borne on by a sort of intoxication, a bravery that whips up your blood, and which surely comes from far back, from your unknown ancestors, from a long past of wars. And then, above all, you have to save your own skin, and that instinct, my lad, keeps you up to the mark.

"No, I am talking of the times when no fighting is going on; when, on the contrary, you are dreading the coming battle, and yet have to be ready for it. It is then that you have ample leisure to reflect. In spite of yourself you take to wondering at the motives of your actions, motives that at times compel you to act. I confess that when I went back to the Army after some years of civilian life, I had pretty well lost the habit of doing so.

"I served many years in Algeria; I won my commission as second-lieutenant in the Crimea, then I was promoted captain on retiring in 1865. All my life has been spent in a disciplined army. No, I never had any trouble in obeying orders, for I had good officers. Anyhow, if I did occasionally grouse at an order—strictly to myself—I did not refuse to obey, because those who gave me the command had the right to do so. They were most truly my superiors, either through seniority or through greater talents and education.

"Afterwards, when I retired, I took to the life of a peace-loving man of the middle class. Those were mighty happy years I spent then, in my dear little townlet of Fondettes, where I had a little house and a little garden, and the 'Three Kings' Inn, where I used to play bowls on Sundays. I used to recall the past pleasantly to enjoy the present. Then, suddenly the future crashed on me like a bolt out of the blue. I still go nowadays, on Sundays, to play bowls at the 'Three Kings,' but the landlord is not the man I once knew, and on the white wall of the inn you can see the twelve holes made by the Prussian bullets that shot down his predecessor.

"But I am wandering. Where had I got to? Ah, yes, I remember: the surprise I felt, the sensation of strangeness when, after the terrible shocks caused by the news of Woerth and Gravelotte, and somewhat later the shameful catastrophe of Sedan, I found myself back in the Army again just as of yore. No, I am wrong; it was not as of yore; all was changed.

"In point of fact there was not an Army any longer. The old Army had vanished. Fifty thousand men were sleeping their last sleep away yonder —all along the frontier, in the ditches by the roadside, in the graves in the fields. A hundred thousand more had just marched past, beaten and cowed, in front of the Prussian eagles: a hundred and fifty thousand more were soon to do the same, leaving Metz standing, full of guns and colors.

"As for Paris, no one knew what was going to happen there, but we kept on hoping. The city was impregnable: first-class generals were there training numerous troops to fighting-pitch: mere rumor perhaps, but it encouraged our morale. But in the provinces, at Tours, what a mess! The Cabinet Ministers were settled permanently there: full of the most absurd confidence one day, and plunged the next into the most ghastly despondency, just as news was good or bad. The news! Enough to drive any one crazy, contradictory as it was, coming in shoals and always false. The newspapers hysterical, the departmental administrations crazed and upset. And with it all, the public, strolling along the streets, laughing, chatting, struck by the novelty of the situation, and finding in it food for amusement.

"Meanwhile, the so-called Army was nothing but a huge multitude in the process of being organized.

In the towns there was an endless mingling of incongruous uniforms: officers of every branch of the service: Garibaldines, Pontifical Zouaves, Territorials and gaily-colored *francs-tireurs*. By the side of brand-new, gold-laced uniforms, other uniforms patched and in rags. And Red Cross men, enough of them to justify the belief that there were more stretcher-bearers and doctors than men. In the camps, a dirty, undisciplined infantry, composed of old soldiers scooped up from anywhere, or else of beardless lads: Territorials who did not know how to handle their weapons: these often no more than old breech-loaders; very little cavalry, very ill-horsed: an insignificant number of guns, with wretched teams. And the whole lot equipped anyhow and insufficiently fed and provisioned.

"But the worst of all was the corps of officers. There was no uniformity, no fusion. The officers were either too old or too young. Some, like myself, white-bearded crocks; others, men from anywhere: business men, lawyers or else mere whipper-snappers with scarce a hair on their lips. I cannot, though three years have gone by, utter that word 'whipper-snapper,' I cannot think of it without feeling my hand tremble and my eyes fill with tears.

"I spoke just now of the trying times that come occasionally to a soldier in the course of his service. Well, the remembrance of one of the most painful of those times is bound up for me in that word—so inoffensive apparently—'whipper-snapper.' It is of the evils of a hierarchy formed at haphazard, of the inevitable relaxation of the bonds of discipline, of the indispensable need for its maintenance, and of

the soul-problems which may result, that I was thinking when I sorrowfully alluded to 'trying times.'

"We had just been beaten at Toury and d'Arte-
nay; Orleans was in the hands of the Bavarians, and
General de la Motte-Rouge had just passed over his
command to General d'Aurelles de Paladine, Gam-
betta having superseded the former. So we were
concentrated, the whole of the 15th Army Corps, in
the camp at Salbris. We spent a fortnight there
which, hardened old soldier that I was, and accustomed to the regularity of duties, was terribly
fatiguing. From morning to night we had to organ-
ize, to create, to superintend, to drill and train the
men. That, however, did not matter much to us:
the hard part was to impress on these men, who had
never had it taught them, or who, having once
learned, had forgotten it—which is worse—the strict
sense of the blind respect for discipline.

"It happened that in camp I met one of my
friends. In the old days we had been non-commis-
sioned officers together at Setif. I, an old junior
in the Zouaves; he a newly-joined artilleryman. We
were glad to meet, I can tell you. He knew me at
once, and we embraced each other in spite of the
difference of rank, for he was still a non-com., having
merely served his time. He told me his whole story:
he was now settled in Marseilles: he was married,
and had a family. Quite happy, he was only forty,
and he had made his pile almost. Of his children,
one was nine years old, and the other, a little girl,
seven, with her mother's lovely blue eyes and long,
fair hair.

"The poor chap was called Poulot. He was such

a good fellow, beloved by all his comrades, always ready with the word of hope or encouragement—a good, quick worker and a first-rate comrade. But the pity of it was that his battery was commanded by a very youthful captain, who had passed through the Central School of Gunnery, and who was as much of a soldier as the Pope. All the same, a sharp, autocratic look, and a dry, insolent way of giving orders. He sneered at the oldest gunners, and treated like a dog even an old and reliable non-com. So one day when he gave an order that struck Poulot as idiotic, Poulot lost patience, shrugged his shoulders and murmured: 'Whipper-snapper!'

"He was at once put under arrest, taken to the cells and then before a court-martial. There was no fooling just then: orders were imperative and severe; they had to be, of course. I saw a boy of eighteen, who had volunteered, and who, his enthusiasm having evaporated, had tried to bolt, I saw him condemned to death. I saw men condemned to be shot for stealing a hen, a turkey—and then I think of the unpunished stragglers who deserted in hundreds! And of pillage and murder sanctioned at other times!

"Well, Poulot was duly shot. I learned of his blunder and his doom at one and the same time. It was but three days before that I had seen him bright, happy, in fine health. I confess that much as I love the Army, much as I love France, soldier through and through though I am, the day on which that piece of news made my heart stop beating, I lost all love of life, and my sword seemed to me to be no less horrible than a murderer's knife. I asked myself, shuddering with revolt and anguish, whether the cult of discipline was always intelligently understood, and whether—blind and deaf god that it is—it had the right to exact such sacrifices."

PIERRE MILLE

XXIII

NUMBER THIRTEEN

By Pierre Mille

FROM time to time Elise Herminier woke up because sharp surges of sudden pain passed through the lower part of her back; it was the muscles getting into place again after her confinement; the doctor had warned her that it would be so. The anguish which made breathing difficult, causing her heart to beat painfully, bringing the sweat to her forehead, did not alarm her; the worst was over, for the baby was there, alive and well beside her. She had only to put out her hand to touch him.

Out of the money she had earned going out as a daily help, Elise had been able to save enough to prepare the indispensable baby-clothes, but nothing for a cradle; and the little one slept close by her in the narrow bed of which a kindly neighbor had just hurriedly changed the sheets. If she had possessed more strength, she would have loved to unswathe him, to see his arms, his legs, his tiny body, so that she might feast her eyes on the wonderful mystery that confused her thoughts . . . that she, a woman, had been able to make a little man!

The room was very small; it was a very hot day, and to give her more air they had left her door wide open, a door on which No. 13 was painted in black letters. Without moving her head, Elise could see a tiled passage broken at regular intervals by brown rectangles indicating other doors marked in a like manner: the monotonous and dreary sight peculiar to the sixth floor of the poorer houses in Paris. Elise knew all those who came every night to sleep there for a few hours; a district watchman, all the servants of the house, a dressmaker, and a gray-haired, bent, old woman who occupied No. 16, four doors along, and who was the envy of every one on that floor because she was ending her days in peace with an income of six hundred francs a year left her by a former employer.

"It's very strange she hasn't been in to see me," thought Elise; "she who has nothing to do."

And when the doctor came in, accompanied by the dressmaker, she asked:

"Do you know, Mademoiselle Emmeline, what Madame Granchet's doing? She's always been so kind."

The dressmaker felt a creeping in her spine. She turned away her head. Madame Granchet had died suddenly during the night; it had been some sort of fit, and they had known nothing about it till they found her stiff and cold in the morning. That was not the kind of news to tell a woman who had just come through a difficult confinement. Besides, the lower classes have generally a fear of death, a simple and reverent fear. Mademoiselle Emmeline had been congratulating herself that her attendance on Elise was a very excellent excuse for not "watching" by the dead woman; others must undertake that office.

She looked at the doctor.

"Madame Granchet is ill," he said.

"In bed?" asked Elise.

"Yes, in her bed."

He spoke in a voice he purposely made indifferent, and began to examine her; it was better to change the conversation. Elise was at that moment seized with one of her fits of pain. Her face blanched, her mouth gaped as do those of little birds when they are dying. But it only lasted a moment; some color came back, and she smiled. He auscultated her, his ear on her heart, his face grave. Elise was no longer thinking of herself, for the baby at her side stirred and made little noises like a kitten mewing.

"It's a fine child, isn't it?" she asked.

"Yes," said the doctor, "a very fine child."

He gave it some sugared water. The whimper ceased. You only heard the almost imperceptible sound of the uncertain little tongue sucking instinctively at the metal spoon. Elise listened, languid, and very happy. He went out into the passage, and the dressmaker followed him.

"Is she going on all right?" she asked.

"Her heart is not sound," he answered, "and she has had some hemorrhage. Beyond that, it's just an ordinary confinement. She'll get over it right enough if nothing unforeseen happens. She must be kept very quiet, no emotion, that's all. Better not let her know that her neighbor is dead . . ."

He went away looking up his next visit in his appointment-book. The doctors of the poor have not much time to lose, especially for confinements paid for out of the public funds.

"Let her have plenty of air. Leave the door open," were his parting words.

Mademoiselle Emmeline came back, bringing her work with her, and sitting near the window so as to get as much light as possible, for the daylight was fading, bent her head over her sewing; and the old maid told herself that there were many compensations for never having had anything to do with men. What would become of her, this Elise Herminier? She had got to earn her living by going out cleaning; how could she do it with this child, that she refused to abandon, in her arms? The father had disappeared: a footman in a house where she had worked occasionally, who had left his place and disappeared so as to avoid the responsibility. Eternal and hackneyed story!

Elise shut her eyes and tried to sleep. She had now a touch of fever, and was shivering. It is easy to protect rich patients and those who are looked after in hospitals from this; but with poor women, who cling tenaciously to tradition, prejudice and superstition, and insist on having their children in their own homes . . . it is not possible. Invisible and dangerous microbes, left by sick or dirty people, for ever lurk about these neglected habitations. They penetrate lungs weakened by hardship, poison the morning cup of milk, contaminate the wound of childbirth. It is inevitable, and as the patient does not always die, the state of affairs continues.

Slowly a kind of delirium crept through Elise's brain. It took the form of terror, for the laboring heart affected the mind, and the young mother's joy gave way to fears which agonized her, and in their turn completed the vicious circle by increasing the palpitation. Why had she not destroyed this germ that was now a man and wanted to live? How could she support him, how could she herself live, with him to look after and keep? Over and over again she counted up the sums she could earn without her weakened brain being able to grasp them; two hours every morning at Madame Dodu's at threepence halfpenny an hour; a whole day every Thursday at Madame Renou's. On Sundays, alas, nobody wanted her. Every one in Paris went out on Sundays nowadays, even the poorest households. No, she couldn't manage it; there was no way of getting money enough for the two. . . . And if she fell ill? . . . Then it would be immediate starvation; no savings to fall back on, nothing but debt. And if she died? Ah! She was going to die; she was sure of it; she was going to die! At these thoughts, it seemed as if her heart was being pinched, twisted round, and it beat with a noise like that of a drum against her chest. She was dying! She could see herself, all white, wrapped round in a white sheet in the bottom of a coffin, while her baby, blue with hunger, cried alone in bed.

*   *   *   *   *   *   *

At this moment two undertaker's men passed before the concierge's lodge in the courtyard of the house, carrying something long covered with black cloth.

"It's for Madame Granchet's room," they explained.

"The back stairs, sixth floor, passage to the right,

number sixteen," said the concierge, who understood.

They went up. It was late. They had been drinking. At the top of the staircase, having stopped to take breath, they turned to the right, and one of them asked:

"What number did they say downstairs?"

"Thirteen," replied the other.

"Thirteen or sixteen?"

The other hesitated:

"Blowed if I know now. Them ' 'teens,' it's easy to mix them up! . . . But we shall see; the door'll likely be open. There'll be some one watching the corpse."

"It's No. 13 right enough. The door's open, and some one's there. . . . The corpse is there, too; you can see it."

The dressmaker had fallen asleep in the window, her sewing in her hand, while, in the shadow thrown by the door, Elise Herminier lay stretched out full length in bed, wrestling with the terrifying thoughts that filled her weak head.

The two black-dressed men walked slowly in, and with deliberation placed their burden on the tiled floor.

"Here's the coffin," they announced as they straightened themselves. One of them had removed the black cloth, and the other held the screws in his hand.

Elise opened her eyes, saw the men, the black cloth, the coffin, and the screws. The coffin! What! Was it really for her? What! She tried to cry out: not a sound came from her mouth. She tried to move: not a stir; she was paralyzed. The only part of her left alive was her heart, which, for one second, gave her atrocious agony. Then nothing more. The dressmaker, waking up, ran to her:

"Madame Elise! Madame Elise!"

A whimper from the baby was the only answer.

*　　*　　*　　*　　*　　*　　*

Thus died Elise Herminier, unmarried mother.

MARCEL PRÉVOST

XXIV

MY BROTHER GUY

By MARCEL PREVOST

[*From* MADAME LAROCHE-THIEBAULT (*widow*) *to*
MADAME D'EPRUN]

WHAT is the latest gossip in Bourges, my Colette? What's been happening since I left a
week ago? Is our little circle of madcaps still engaged in scandalizing the moldy provincial town
where military duties and arranged marriages have
collected them? Has the olive-skinned Comtesse de
Prenilly unearthed any more eighteenth-century
songs, whose libertine sentiments come sweetly from
her pure mouth? Has the Colonel's wife succeeded
in getting up a quarrel with the nice young Second-
Lieutenant Saint Remi, fresh from Vaugirard?
Do our men-friends still treat you as if they were
hussars; and you, do you still behave as if you were
light young women? What a stupid place! No matter how one tries to deceive oneself, what efforts
one makes to persuade oneself that one is having a
gay time there, it is always Bourges the Melancholy,
asleep in the shadow of its cathedral. . . . I had
had enough, so much too much of the good town
that the other evening I took the last train for Paris
without telling any one. Hurrah, for the indepen-

dence of widowhood! Let me be frank: it was not only boredom that I ran away from. I had been imprudent enough to promise a rendezvous for next day to Captain d'Exiles! Yes, at my house, a rendezvous . . . And though that sort of thing seems charming and amusing when you think about it at a safe distance, it's very different when the moment comes to put it into execution. There's nobody at home! Funny, isn't it? I'd rather go and listen to a long and tedious sermon. I imagine we're all a bit like that. Always ready to talk about such things, but never in earnest if it comes to doing them.

Well, there I was in the train, rushing towards Paris in the darkness, hugging myself with joy at the thought that d'Exiles, after having perfumed and curled himself, and generally prepared for my conquest, would appear smiling at the door of my house next day. In imagination I saw the bland expression on the face of Solange, my maid. "Madame requested me to tell Monsieur le Capitaine that she was extremely sorry. . . . Madame has been obliged to leave for Paris to see her brother . . . family affairs . . ." And I could hear the swear words uttered by Monsieur le Capitaine as he returned to barracks.

The men of his company would probably have rather a bad time of it on parade the next few days!

There was some truth in what Solange had said. I really did drive straight to my brother's when I got to Paris. Guy has a wonderful flat in the rue des Ecuries-d'Artois, and its arrangement is . . . a woman of really good taste has certainly been there; one, or several!

When I was leaving Bourges I had scribbled off a telegram: "Expect me to-night about eleven o'clock." It was striking half-past as I entered his delightful rooms. Guy was in his dressing-room putting the last touches to his white evening tie under the anxious scrutiny of his valet.

"What on earth have you come to do in Paris in such a hurry?" he said to me.

"My dear Guy, don't scold me," I answered. "I was bored to death in Bourges."

"There's no doubt that twelve months every year at Bourges . . . but you don't mean to put up here, I suppose?"

"For to-night, yes . . . To-morrow I will look out for rooms."

Guy seemed to be taken aback. . . . My arrival was evidently disturbing his arrangements for the evening. But as he is really nice and very fond of his younger sister, he made light of it.

"Right; that's understood, my room shall be got ready for you, and I . . . I will sleep somewhere else . . . at a friend's. . . . But I warn you I shall leave you to-night for supper."

"Oh! Guy . . . and I was so happy . . . Do you mean to leave me all alone when I have hardly even arrived?"

"I can't take you with me. I am going into a set where young widows are not admitted."

His valet had discreetly withdrawn. I went up to Guy and said with a smile:

"Are you going out to supper with some young woman?"

"Precisely."

"Ladies and gentlemen?"

"Only one man. You don't know him. A Roumanian whom I met at Bucharest ... Count Ildescu."

"And who are the young ladies?"

"Lucienne d'Argenson, Fanny Love and la belle Cordoba. I hope you'll believe that it's not for my own pleasure. They bore me to death. But Ildescu was set on knowing them, so I am presenting all three of them together to stop his worrying me any more."

"Well . . . take me with you . . ."

I didn't leave Guy time to protest. I sat down on his knee and wheedled him; I explained to him that I was in exactly the same position as Ildescu; that Bourges was much more depressing than Bucharest, and that I, too, like Ildescu, was dying to see Fanny Love, Lucienne d'Argenson and la belle Cordoba.

"But look here, this is rank madness. If any one were to recognize you . . ."

"I will put on a thick veil until we reach the private dining-room. . . . After that there is no danger. Neither your friend nor these young ladies have ever seen me."

"But perhaps they will say some rather risky things . . ."

"Bah! I am not a raw young girl. . . . Besides if they go too far you can take me away."

In short, as time was flying, and I would not give in, Guy let himself be persuaded. It was agreed that I should pretend to be a young amateur from the provinces, a friend of Guy's, about to start a career in Paris. I had a very nice evening-dress in my trunk, and I dressed myself as smartly as I could: Guy acted as my lady's maid. My idea began to amuse him, even him.

"By Jove," he said to me when I was ready, "you look a jolly sight better than those old birds we are going to meet. Ildescu will lose his head. Take care! He's a dangerous fellow."

We were to have supper at Joseph's; the time was to be one o'clock, as Fanny Love and la belle Cordoba were not free until the theaters were over. Count Ildescu had undertaken to call for Lucienne d'Argenson at her house. We arrived, my brother and I, a quarter of an hour late—the last.

Oh! that look, my Colette! the triple survey of these three women who started gauging me, judging me from the moment that Guy introduced me as "Mademoiselle Renée . . . of Châtellerault . . . who has just arrived in Paris." No compliment has ever flattered me so much as that simultaneous look of antagonism on those three pretty faces (for really they are quite lovely, these creatures), and the annoyance they could not hide at finding me as pretty as they were! . . . They made up for it over my toilette. I heard them making fun of it, whilst Ildescu, already very much taken with me, was overwhelming me with politenesses.

To tell the truth, they were more fashionably dressed than I was, and would you believe it, just as correctly, with a refined and sober elegance, in perfect taste . . . We sat down to supper: I was placed between Ildescu and Mlle. d'Argenson. Supper began. I drank two glasses of champagne straight off, and immediately I felt at my ease and prepared to listen to anything.

At first they spoke about the theaters. Fanny Love and la belle Cordoba gave us their impressions of contemporary dramatic art: they seemed to me to be much better informed and hardly more shallow-minded than the ladies of our aristocracy. Then Lucienne d'Argenson launched forth into her ideas about society, the life of the smart set and the reduction of incomes: in twenty years, she said, there would be no rich people left in Paris. I recognized the last sentence from having heard it uttered several times by the wife of our chief treasurer. Guy listened gravely to it all, and answered in the same way. But Ildescu . . . he began whispering nonsense into my ear, and I assure you there is a great deal of difference between his nonsense and the common-places of Monsieur d'Exiles or young Saint Remi, or any of our friends! He limited himself to remarks on my personal appearance, and was most persistent in his admiration; and I, I made a mental comparison between my own physical attractions and those of the three others, and I really felt proud of his preference.

"Up to the present, anyway," I thought to myself, "it's been as dull as a family party! Evidently I am a wet blanket! They think I'm provincial, and silly at that. I'll put them at their ease."

So I drank another glass of champagne, and told them that nice little story of yours, the one we all liked so much when you told it at dinner at the Colonel's the other night; you know the one about the tell-tale confetti. Oh, my Colette! if only you could have seen the expression on the faces of those three young ladies! They pretended they did not understand it! And the disdainful remarks they made to each other when I had finished! Guy, red as a poppy, thought it right to make excuses for me to his neighbor, Fanny Love: "You see she doesn't quite understand. . . . Later on she'll have learnt how to behave . . ." But Ildescu, he laughed with all his heart: "Ah! how funny! very funny! very amusing! very Parisian! she is adorable!" And suddenly I felt his knee trying to enter into conversation with mine under the table. That worried me; I don't approve of gentlemen giving themselves such privileges without asking permission! But I reflected that it was perhaps just part of the performance, and that if I protested, they would guess that I didn't belong to the profession. So Ildescu did not meet with more resistance than was necessary, till suddenly we heard the shrill voice of Fanny Love exclaiming, as she rapped Guy sharply over the knuckles with her fan:

"Tell me, my dear man, will it be long before you've finished spoiling my dress with your feet? Where do you think you are? At Châtellerault?"

"At Châtellerault"—that was for me. I understood, and quickly shrank into myself much to the regret of Ildescu, who rolled his fine black eyes with surprise and disappointment. . . . Supper came to an end almost in silence: Lucienne and la belle Cordoba were the only ones who talked; and they discoursed about gold-mines. We left about half-past two. The three ladies bid me the coldest of good-bys. They were seen into their cars: Ildescu was quite determined to accompany me.

"Hold on, my dear chap," said Guy. "I'm going to see Madame home."

Poor Roumanian Count! He looked so downcast I let him squeeze my fingers as long as he liked when we shook hands.

As soon as I was alone with Guy in his coupé, I made a scene.

"You will never get me to believe this is one of your ordinary supper-parties, what you call having a good time! You told those three sirens who I was, and the whole thing was spoilt. And I should have enjoyed myself so much!"

He defended himself with energy:

"I give you my word that all our little parties are very much like this one. Now and again a quarrel or an attack of nerves—that's the most exciting thing that ever happens . . . otherwise, 'having a good time' is just what you've seen. Amusing, isn't it? But what would you have us do? One must pass the evenings somehow."

"But surely they are not always as . . . proper, these young ladies? . . . I suppose that when you are alone together . . ."

"Ah!" replied Guy smiling, "naturally, when you are alone with them, it's quite another matter. For them, that's work—work they're paid for; and they take good care not to work for nothing in off-hours . . . For these women, 'Love' is business."

It seemed to me that this explanation of my brother Guy was worth thinking about, and when I was in bed, I meditated long on it. And I can

assure you, my Colette, that my thoughts were of
extreme morality. There can't be much amusement
in having to go through love-scenes with any sort of
Ildescu who happens to sit next you at supper! Poor
women! And to think that other women sometimes
almost envy them! How well I understand now
their playing the part of decent women when they're
not at business, just as we others play at being gay
women in our leisure in the provinces!

*   *   *   *   *   *   *

I'm going back to Bourges next Tuesday. My
regards to Monsieur d'Exiles. He is decidedly
preferable to the Roumanian. Talking of the Roumanian, what do you think? When I opened the
Journal this morning I came across this in the personal column:

"A young man, dark, rich, having supped at
Joseph's with a delightful person from Châtellerault
is very anxious to see her again.—I."

"I." must be Ildescu!

So of the four of us, Fanny Love, Cordoba,
d'Argenson and I, it was I who "got" the Roumanian—I, the amateur!

MICHEL PROVINS

XXV

"GOSSIP"

By Michel Provins

*A*T *Aix-les-Bains. Place: The Gardens of the Villa des Fleurs. Time: The hour when people lounge about and watch each other; the hour for flirtation and the display of costumes; the hour when the hot-bed of society produces its most poisonous scandals.*

On the lawns with their mosaic of geraniums there is the flutter of sensational toilettes, the clash of discordant colors, the glitter of jewels in the full sunlight, all the carnival of luxury and pleasure that too often cloaks lies and infirmities.

In the bandstand an orchestra is playing a senti-mental waltz of the erotico-Wagnerian kind.

One of the groups is particularly animated. La Brette—the well-informed man-of-the-world—is lay-ing down the law with an assurance born of complete vacuity of mind, and he is being listened to with great attention by the cosmopolitan men and women who surround him.

DE LYEUSE. I say, La Brette, you know every-body; who is that pretty woman over there, walking with the man in the pepper-and-salt suit?

LA BRETTE (*looking*). That is the beautiful Madame Deguerny, the mistress of Rambert.

MADAME AREGGIO. What, Rambert, the ex-Minister?

LA BRETTE. Himself! . . . the powerful orator; the great man of the Central Party. He never leaves her.

MADAME DE ST. LEGER (*peering through her lorgnettes*). A little coarse, the favored one.

LA BRETTE. What do you expect? For a man who started life in clogs, son of a workman . . .

MADAME AREGGIO (*still peering*). I imagined him to be a younger man.

LA BRETTE. Forty-six. Fifteen years older than . . . his friend . . .

DE LYEUSE. Is there a Monsieur Deguerny?

VAREUIL. Very much so . . . one of our youngest and most highly-placed officials. Légion d'Honneur and Head of his Department . . . and all in ten years.

LA BRETTE (*with a supercilious smile*). The exact time the liaison has lasted.

DE LYEUSE. And how long have they been married?

LA BRETTE. Just eleven years.

MADAME AREGGIO. Good heavens! Then he, the husband, must be shutting his eyes to it.

LA BRETTE. One never can tell. Fate sometimes afflicts husbands with sublime blindness . . . But in this case it is difficult to believe it. Rambert's intimacy is so close, and the favors he bestows so notorious.

VAREUIL. But, all the same, Deguerny is looked upon as a man of remarkable talent in his department.

LA BRETTE. Yes . . . Very well up in his subject. Very stern, and a stickler for the virtues. Always a good pose for a man in his . . . conjugal position.

VAREUIL. Excuse me, you speak of this as if it were a matter of public notoriety; is it so?

LA BRETTE. Of course it is. Everybody knows it just as everybody knows that the Arc de Triomphe is at the top of the Champs Elysées . . . Ask in any drawing-room in Paris "Who is Madame Deguerny?" and you will be told: "The mistress of Rambert."

VAREUIL. But you have seen it? (LA BRETTE *does not grasp his meaning.*) Yes, have you seen this adultery for which you vouch so categorically?

LA BRETTE (*taken aback*). I've never been called in to watch it! . . . (*general laughter*) but as I have heard it talked about for ten years . . .

VAREUIL. There are many calumnies that have been current for longer than that.

LA BRETTE. Agreed . . . but if you had watched the trio as closely as I have . . .

DE LYEUSE. What? Do you know Deguerny?

LA BRETTE (*blandly*). Do I know him? . . . Why, Deguerny and I were at college together, and I dine with them once a week.

VAREUIL (*sarcastically*). I thought from the way you talked that you must be an intimate friend of his.

*   *   *   *   *   *   *

Coming back together from the other side of the garden, Aline Deguerny and Rambert run the gaunt-

let of another group that is discussing them, the
young woman being too pretty and the man too cele-
brated to avoid provoking ill-natured criticism.

ALINE (*sitting down*). Did you hear?

RAMBERT (*irritably*). Yes, the eternal poisonous
and silly remarks! What vile minds most people
have . . . always beginning by imputing evil motives, and never conceding that any one else can have
a pure or disinterested one. Intimacy? Then adultery. Riches and success? Gained by compromise,
blackmail or unfair bargaining. That's their standard of judgment. As for admitting that there could
be pure friendship between a man and a woman, that
would be too simple and too beautiful a thought to
enter their heads . . . the distillers of poison would
get nothing out of it!

ALINE. Don't pay any attention to them. We
inspire too much envy in people like that for them to
spare us. You are a distinguished man, head and
shoulders above the others, and I am a woman of
independent character, disdaining hypocritical preju-
dices and senseless conventions; I don't associate
with many women; I talk to the men as if they were
comrades; I dress well, and I go about openly with
you! It's more than enough to make them flay us
alive.

RAMBERT. But you are forgetting the last cause
for a chorus of calumnies—the promotion that is
entirely due to your husband's qualities.

ALINE. Oh, let them lie! Let them chatter as
they like. How can their inventions affect us? We
know the truth, and that is enough.

RAMBERT. Do you really believe that that is

enough? (*A movement of surprise from Aline.*)
Yes, every time I hear an echo of what they say
about us, I wonder if we are right to defy public
opinion. In spite of how much I should miss you,
perhaps it would be better not to see you so often,
not to appear so intimate with you, or go so often
to your house.

ALINE. And you really think that would stop
their yapping out their famous: "The beautiful
Madame Deguerny, the mistress of Rambert"?

RAMBERT. In time they would forget to say it.
. . . Yes, I am beginning to believe that I shall
have to keep away from you, for your sake . . . for
your husband's.

ALINE. But I tell you it doesn't matter at all
to me. As for George . . .

RAMBERT. Do you think he knows what they
say?

ALINE. I think so . . . It is such common talk
. . . But as he is highly intelligent, very just, adores
me, likes you, and is quite sure of us both, he attaches no importance to it. He is not the kind of
man who would mention it to me; if he knows, he is
silent because he would think it beneath his dignity
to allude to it.

RAMBERT. But suppose he knows nothing of
those libels, and should hear them suddenly by chance
or from some motive of revenge? Might it not have
an extraordinary effect on a character like his? He
is so straightforward—so rigid. Wouldn't it be
better and safer to prepare him by telling him just
how things are?

ALINE (*almost angry*). What? Tell him the

whole story? Betray Mother? Surely you realize that we can't explain without sacrificing her honor? Impossible.

RAMBERT. Humiliating for you and for me, but not impossible.

ALINE. But Mother? Are you forgetting our promise to her? Is it possible to break a promise made to a dying person?

RAMBERT. I am not forgetting anything, therefore I remember that she added: "Unless your happiness is at stake."

ALINE. That's true. (*A pause, then reflecting.*) What an extraordinary scene. I was only thirteen, but every time I think of it I can see it all as clearly as if it were before me. I can hear Mother's voice, the slow, faint voice of the dying: "Aline, my darling, you will be all alone. . . . I must tell you . . . I must confess my sin . . . the only great sin of my life. . . . Lucien"—you were kneeling close beside me—"Lucien Rambert is your brother . . . yes . . . yes . . . your brother . . . his father, our late employee, the manager at the works, was my lover . . . and you are his daughter . . . so Lucien is your brother . . . they are both dead, your real father and the other . . . and I am dying too . . . Are you listening, Lucien? Remember what I say . . . you owe all you are and will be to me. . . . I have paid for your education . . . your start in life . . . you will become a man of note . . . take care of your sister . . . my Aline . . . she will have no one but you. . . . Love him, Aline, and trust him . . . your love for him will absolve me of my sin . . ." Poor little Mother! . . .

RAMBERT (*taking her hand*). And have I not done all I could to fulfil my promise?

ALINE. Indeed you have. You have been wonderfully good to me. There was hardly any money left, and you smoothed everything for me, and when you became rich and powerful, you gave me a dowry and arranged my marriage . . . And you think we can tell George this after having hidden it from him all these years?

RAMBERT. Why not? He would understand . . .

ALINE. Would he? Understand our silence and the way we have deceived him? He believes he married the legitimate daughter of my mother, with a fortune of her own. Why risk such a test when it's not necessary to do so? Time enough if it ever becomes impossible to avoid it .

RAMBERT. Perhaps you are right.

ALINE. I'm certain I am. The years go by quietly and happily, and the past is dead. Don't let us risk spoiling the present. . . . And there is something very charming in this long complicity of affection, in being brother and sister and appearing to be lovers. . . . Suppose we told our story, do you know what people would say?

RAMBERT. *Se non è vero, è ben' trovato?* . . .

ALINE. Exactly! They wouldn't believe us, so what would be the good?

RAMBERT. Yes, you're right. Let us continue to live our lives our own way, fixing our thoughts on beautiful things. . . . Look, little sister, at those mountains! Aren't they wonderful, all tinged with the heliotrope and gold of the evening light? How beautiful nature is . . .

ALINE.   And how different from the mind of man!

*   *   *   *   *   *   *

In a quiet part of the garden, Deguerny, who has been waiting half-an-hour for the opportunity, suddenly appears before La Brette as he comes out of the gambling-rooms.

DEGUERNY (*very pale, but master of himself*). I've been looking for you. I've got something to say to you.

LA BRETTE (*taken aback by Deguerny's tone*). To me? . . . What's the matter? . . . Anything wrong? . . .

DEGUERNY.   I was passing behind those shrubs some time ago; you were talking loudly to a dozen people, and I heard you say, "the beautiful Madame Deguerny, the mistress of Rambert."

LA BRETTE (*stammering*).   You didn't catch the words properly.

DEGUERNY.   Don't lie! La Brette (*going close to him and speaking in icy tones*) what you said was either an infamous lie for which you shall give me satisfaction; or else the fact is so well-known that you, my friend, repeated it without realizing that it was a cowardly betrayal. Which is it? . . . In the latter case, I shall not hold you responsible . . . I shall leave you to pass judgment on yourself.

LA BRETTE (*at his wits' end, and playing for time*).   Listen to me . . .

DEGUERNY.   I want no explanations. It is one thing or the other . . . Answer me! As you see, I am quite calm, and I swear that no one but myself

shall suffer for what you are going to tell me . . .
You see you are free to tell the truth.

La Brette (*to himself*). Is he in earnest? What
does he really mean?

Deguerny (*threatening*). Answer me! Did
you invent this?

La Brette (*stupefied*). You are forcing me into
an awful position. I admit I have been tactless,
foolish . . . but you know how it is when you get
talking . . . you let yourself go, you repeat things
without reflecting, without any thought of evil . . .

Deguerny (*growing still paler*). "Repeat
things"—then people do say that Madame Deguerny is the mistress of Rambert? Do they say
that?

La Brette (*cowering*). I am not responsible
for other people, and—yes—they do say that!

Deguerny (*trembling*). Since when?

La Brette (*not knowing what to say*). That is
going too far.

Deguerny. Too far? Then I'll get corrobora-
tion. (*He sees* De Lyeuse *who is passing by, and
whom he does not know, and raises his voice*). Excuse me, Sir . . .

La Brette (*springing forward to prevent conversation*). No!

Deguerny. You see . . . you are certain of his
reply; of the answer of the first passer-by, even here
in the country . . . But you? . . . You who saw me
every day, who saw Aline and Rambert, what did
you think of them, of me?

La Brette (*imbecile*). I thought you knew . . .

either you were sure there was nothing, or you knew and were making the best of it.

DEGUERNY (*bursting into a nervous laugh that sounds more like the agonized cry of a tortured soul*). How well you understand my character! Naturally I have been making the best of it . . . I only wanted to make you talk! . . .

LA BRETTE (*at a loss to understand, watches him uneasily as he tears a page from a pocket-book and begins writing on it*). What are you going to do?

DEGUERNY (*quite master of himself again*). A little joke . . . a surprise! . . . It's better to laugh than to be angry, isn't it? (*Continues to write.*) You will deliver this little note to my wife this evening. I shall not be in to dinner.

LA BRETTE. Where are you going?

DEGUERNY. For a row on the lake.

LA BRETTE. As late as this? . . . alone?

DEGUERNY. Yes, alone. Evening on the lake— nothing like it for refreshing your mind. (*Having finished writing, he folds the paper and hands it to him.*) There! . . . Give it to Aline . . . but not before ten o'clock, otherwise it won't fit in with the little surprise I wish to give her . . . Good evening! (*And before La Brette has time to muster his wits or utter a word, he has reached the street and disappeared.*)

*　　*　　*　　*　　*　　*　　*

Well before the appointed time, but already too late, La Brette meets Aline and Rambert together in the hotel. They are both feeling anxious about the inexplicable absence of Deguerny.

La Brette (*delivering the note*). From your husband.

Aline (*amazed*). What? . . . A letter? . . . (*Opening it.*) "My dear Aline, as you have been the mistress of Rambert so long, why not become his wife?" (*At the exclamation that seems to tear her throat, Rambert rushes forward and reads out loud with her, oblivious of the presence of* La Brette.) "By the time you get this note, it will be useless to look for me. I am going where nobody can find me. I did not wish to see you again because I love you too dearly, because never having suspected how things were, I should, in spite of all evidence to the contrary, be too afraid of believing your denials. By disappearing, I absolve myself in public opinion from the sin of my supposed complaisance, and I give you a chance of rehabilitating yourself. Thank you for the illusion of happiness you have given me . . . and as I shall no longer be alive to suffer, I forgive you."

Overwhelmed by the suddenness of the tragedy, the brother and sister look at each other in silence, trembling; then impelled by the instinct that makes human beings seek consolation in moments of mental anguish in physical contact, Aline throws herself into the arms Rambert instinctively holds out to her.

La Brette (*thunderstruck, his despicable brain incapable of seeing anything but confirmation of the scandal in this action*). My God! Talk about shamelessness! (*Then hurrying away to have the pleasure of being the first to spread the savory news.*) And men will kill themselves for the sake of women!

J. H. ROSNY, *aîné*

XXVI

THE CHAMPION

By J. H. Rosny, *aîné*

I

WE were chaffing the philosophic Saverre about being so tremendously keen on athletics. Personally, he is delicate, almost puny, all brain and no body to speak of; but he finds an extraordinary pleasure in witnessing any notable match—wrestling, boxing, fencing, or even a trial of mere physical strength. He takes in all the sporting papers, knows the best boxers in France and England, the crack swordsmen, the famous toreadors. He let us have our laugh out, and then told us the origin of these predilections so foreign to his temperament and physique.

"My father," he said, "was a poor man, a widower, whom a series of misfortunes had obliged to take a small post as accountant in a chemical manufactory in a remote country district. This employment, obtained after long months of application, was not very exacting, but was poorly remunerated. But he was only too pleased to get it; deeply embarrassed as he was, he aspired to nothing better, and had no anxiety now but the fear of losing it. The village of S——, where we had to take up our abode, is a comfortless, desolate, unhealthy place surrounded by a barren moor. The inhabitants, quarrelsome and ill-conditioned, have rude aggressive manners, and are by no means prepossessed in favor of strangers. My father was the less welcome inasmuch as his position as a poor gentleman alienated him alike from the peasants and the gentry proper. He recognized this from the first, and determined to occupy himself wholly with his business and to avoid every one. As for myself, regarded as I was with no good-will by the children of the village, I thought it best not to mix with them, nor indeed to venture far beyond the limits of our pine-wood dwelling. Some months passed; and in spite of these discordant elements, the uprightness and kindliness of my father, and a certain light-heartedness which I possessed at that time of my life, procured us a few acquaintances. We were neither happy nor miserable. My father was fond of gardening; and I, already of a contemplative turn of mind, was content enough to dream on waysides or on the skirt of the little wood that bordered our cottage. Two or three times a week I joined in some children's games, and came off without more fisticuffs than might be anticipated.

"But on a certain day this existence became intolerable on account of a family which came to settle in the village, having inherited some acres of grassland, and whose children took part in our sports. One of these, a boy of twelve, thick-set, nimble, with little, fierce, piercing eyes, revealed at once all the characteristics of a tyrant. In a dispute on the bowling-green, he decided in his own favor the position of a ball which we all thought open to question. One of us having protested rather angrily, he knocked him down with a blow on the nose; after which he challenged us with savage effrontery to fight. We were intimidated: the boldest looked at one another doubtfully. However, urged on by all of us, Robert Dubourg, indubitably the strongest and pluckiest of our party, at last accepted the challenge. Alas, the battle was soon over. In less than no time the new-comer had settled our champion and beaten him to pulp. From that time the young tyrant completely dominated us by his bluster and brutality. The matter went so far that one day the father of one of us, a powerful man, whose offspring had been brought home covered with blood, went to demand satisfaction from the father of the assailant.

"It was a day in October—how well I can remember every detail of the scene—a fine warm morning, a little overcast. The man stood before the door of the new-comer's little farm shaking his fist and swearing, and at last gave a furious knock. Instantly the door opened, and there appeared a peasant of moderate height with the little, fierce, piercing eyes of his son. He had also the same look of savage strength.

" 'What do you want?' he said in a husky voice.

" 'I want to give your son a hiding for what he has done to mine.'

" 'Yours ought to have looked out for himself.'

" 'Yours will come to the scaffold.'

" 'Say that again——'

"Davesne's face, coarse, malignant, determined,

was thrust forward into that of the complainant. But the latter was not the sort of man to be easily frightened; he relied, moreover, on his great strength and his courage.

" 'I say your son will come to the scaffold.'

"Hardly had the words passed his lips when a tremendous box on the ear made him stagger, as Davesne cried::

" 'Take that!'

"The man recoiled a pace, clenched his enormous fists, and lowered his head like a bull. Davesne made no motion of avoidance, no parry, good or bad, but sprang at the left shoulder of his man, and seizing his arms, threw him with a sudden jerk to the ground.

" 'Get up . . . I'm going to smash you!'

"The other rose, and more cautious, though undaunted as ever, made two or three feints, and then came on with a rush. He was received in so rough a fashion, with such a rain of blows on his eyes and face generally, that he fell stunned and motionless. And Davesne, in the face of some fifty peasants who had run to the spot, coolly spat upon the face of his defeated enemy, saying:

"That's what I'll do to any one who falls foul of me!'

"Scared by the terrific strength he had displayed, fascinated by his little, malevolent eyes, the peasants stood by motionless. Just then my father appeared. He was white with anger.

" 'This is shameful,' he said sternly.

" 'Eh!' said Davesne. . . . 'What's that the factory-rat says?'

" 'I say it is shameful.'

"The words were hardly out of his mouth before he was caught up from where he stood among the peasants, and placed against the wall of the farmhouse. With quick movements he tried to defend himself. The other felled him with one hand, calmly set a knee on his breast and said:

" 'Beg my pardon.'

" 'No.'

Gasping, mad with rage, I flew to the assistance of my father, and thumped the monster with my fist. Instantly a hand seized and held me in its grip, and before I knew where I was, I was dragged down in my turn and under the knees of Davesne.

"And finding ourselves on the ground, powerless, crushed, choking—and this because we had yielded to a generous impulse—with fifty terrified peasants looking on at a respectful distance, not one of them daring to raise a hand or a voice on our behalf, I realized for the first time in its full meaning the cowardice of human nature, and how easy it is to browbeat and enslave by brute force. The fallen man was the only one who tried to take our part. He raised himself with difficulty, and advanced a few paces; a cunningly-directed kick brought him to the ground again.

"Then Davesne deliberately and repeatedly spat in my father's face, punching him about the body with uncontrolled violence. I made a desperate effort to free myself, and such was my bewildered passion, my frenzied indignation, I did not even notice the blows with which young Davesne assailed me.

"The miserable business ended at last. My father was hurled a dozen paces, beaten black and blue, and I found myself beside him half-strangled with rage, grief and humiliation.

" 'Coward!   Coward!   Coward!' shouted my father.

"With an insulting laugh the bully rushed at him again, and once again my father was on the ground. Then taking his time, Davesne retreated to the door of his cottage, while some women accompanied the limping men to a neighboring tavern: *for not a single man dare appear to take their part.*

II

"You can imagine the deplorable condition of my father during the following days. Every sentiment of human dignity outraged, the excruciating pangs a proud nature suffers when it is subjected to tyranny against which there is no redress, the benumbing effects of sleeplessness, the heart set on fire by sudden rushes of memory in which he lived the scene over again, the contraction of the stomach when he tried to eat, the sensation of the world being upside down, the long gray evenings when he sat silent and somber in the twilight—all this preyed on him physically, and he grew pale and thin.

"He avoided every one, kept in the garden after working hours, never went out unless armed with a long knife, dwelt unceasingly on the misery of his circumstances. As for myself, there was no more play, and the world ended with the garden of our little cottage. Some kind of evil spell seemed to

hang over the village and the desolate moors that
seemed to shut us in.

"But in spite of this seclusion, a fresh humiliation
was in store for us.

"It was Sunday. Though my father was not a
religious man, he sometimes went to Mass out of
respect for the old curé, who was an amiable and
worthy man. On this occasion, when we were
nearing home we found ourselves face to face with
Davesne and his son. My father tried to keep clear
of them, wishing to avoid a second conflict in which
he was resolved to make use of his knife. But
young Davesne did not see matters in that light.
He barred my way, and planting himself in front of
me, hissed in my face.

" 'Little beast,' he muttered with a sneering grin,
as I tried to evade him.

"I was determined not to answer. My silence
enraged him, and he caught me by the ear and
dragged me along. The pain was acute, but I made
no sound; I only tried to get away. Then my father,
who was some paces in front, turned back. He was
deadly pale, and his eye gleamed with a dangerous
brightness.

" 'Let go of him!' he said to young Davesne.

"The boy gave a defiant chuckle, and pulled
harder at my ear. My father took him by the wrist,
and separated his fingers. As I got free a savage
voice growled:

" 'You have laid hands on my boy . . .'

" 'He was ill-treating mine!'

"Never shall I forget the horror of that moment.
Fully aware of his own strength, Davesne gathered

himself up and raised his hand, and my father, *fully aware of his own weakness,* encountered the ferocious eyes of the peasant.

" 'Keep your hands off that son of mine . . . beg his pardon.'

" 'I didn't hurt him in any way.'

" 'Beg his pardon.'

" 'I will not.'

"The huge hand fell and imprinted itself on my father's face. At the same moment there was the gleam of a knife.

" 'So that's your game, is it?' cried Davesne, taking a step back. 'We're going to have some fun.'

"He drew from his pocket a sort of little dagger inclosed in a sheath. The blade was triangular, rather tarnished and oily. As he advanced, my father struck out, but his arm was flung aside, and the little dagger entered his left shoulder. A moment later his knife was snatched from him, and Davesne cried triumphantly:

" 'There, factory rat, you always get what you ask for!'

"My father staggered against the wall, while Davesne, brandishing the captured knife and dagger, looked threateningly at the crowd of peasants who showed some signs of terror-stricken indignation:

" 'And I've got the same waiting for all of you, you pack of cowards!'

III

"From that day the village was so thoroughly subjugated that no one would have dared appear in a court of justice against Davesne. The brute prided himself on his triumph, and accentuated it on every occasion by some truculent action in the tavern or in the open street. The village folk became resigned to it, and some of them even paid a sycophantish court to the conquering hero. As for young Davesne, he was the undisputed king of the boys, bullying them when he was so inclined, and thrashing them at his pleasure. My father and I lived in an atmosphere of shame, horror, revolt, impotence—lived so lonely and isolated that we almost became savages. The idea of justice was dead within us; the world seemed so awful that we many a time wished we were dead.

"In this way a year passed by, and then came the spring morning when a new adventure befell me. I had risked taking a walk through the little wood, and as I returned home, I found myself mixed up with a group of urchins not far from the factory.

"It was on the border of a meadow through which flowed a small stream, little more than a brook. On the right, at a short distance, was a cottage which had been occupied only the day before by a temporary inhabitant, a carpenter by trade, who had come to undertake some additional constructions at the factory. As I came out of the wood I found myself, as I say, confronted by a dozen boys under the leadership of young Davesne.

"The latter had no sooner spied me than he called out:

" 'So it's you, little pig . . . come here!'

"I pretended not to hear and hurried on.

" 'Are you deaf?' shouted the tyrant. 'Come here, I tell you!'

"My heart was beating furiously, but I continued to walk on without saying a word. Then young Davesne, with a bound, caught me up and seized me by the hair.

"'Ah, you won't answer, dirty little beast! You think you're very clever, don't you?'

"I knew that all resistance was useless and only likely to make matters worse. I let myself be dragged along the meadow amid the obsequious laughter of the others, who tried to curry favor with the young monster. Thus we came to the bank of the stream.

"'What if we give him a bath?' said some one.

"'Capital,' assented Davesne. 'We'll see how he likes the taste of water.'

"He still held me roughly by the hair. I knew that he would not scruple to hold my head under the water as long as he liked, and I began to struggle desperately.

"'The calf hangs back, doesn't it?' said Davesne. 'Wait a moment and I'll show you!'

"He had pushed me down, and I was almost touching the water when a clear, bold, young voice broke upon us.

"'What are you doing there?'

"Davesne, surprised, stopped pushing me, and I saw running from the cottage a black-haired, white-skinned boy, whose eyes sparkled with anger. With a bound he was in our midst, and had shoved Davesne roughly aside. It was then that I experienced a mingled emotion, intense and contradictory, such as I have never known before or since—infinite surprise and gratitude, a subtle fondness for the stranger-boy, regret that he should be there, a readiness to suffer myself rather than see him exposed to the brutality of my tormentor.

"'Perhaps you'd like to take a bath instead of him?' sneered Davesne.

"I tried to get between them. Davesne knocked me out of the way with a blow of his fist. The stranger said eagerly:

"'Leave it to me!'

"I would have intervened, whatever the consequences, but two or three of Davesne's toadies held me off. Then I saw the young ruffian rub his hands and lower his head, while the other looked at him taking his measure. There could be no doubt as to the issue of the contest. Although they were nearly equal in size, there was in Davesne something of iron resistance that marked him out for victory.

"As they sprang at each other I shut my eyes, so that I might not see my young champion overthrown. When I opened them again, wondering at the continuance of the battle, I became greatly excited. Davesne had fallen back, visibly hard-pressed, and the other with quick, almost rhythmic movements, was gaining upon him every moment. At one time the battle wavered, at another Davesne seemed to be getting the upper hand, and then all of a sudden, I saw the tyrant on the ground trying to strike and bite, while the other struck him vigorously on the jaw. The frantic joy that took possession of me made me tremble from head to foot. It seemed to me that the whole of life had changed, and that it had become beautiful. Only one pang shot across the felicity of that minute—the fear that Davesne

would take his revenge; and I beheld the conqueror
with eyes of adoration such as I had assuredly never
bestowed upon any symbol of divinity.

"Meanwhile, having thoroughly pressed home his
victory, and pounded the other, as he thought, into
impotence, the stranger leapt to his feet. Davesne
was up almost at the same time, and advancing to
renew the battle.

"'Look out!' I cried in terror.

"I would have got in between them, but my new
friend pushed me away with a: 'Leave it to me!'

"Almost as he spoke, Davesne made a rush with
that rapidity and force which made him irresistible.
My friend jumped back a couple of paces, took a
bound in his turn, and shot like a bullet at his an-
tagonist. Davesne rolled on the ground once more.

"I had no further anxiety. A joyful sense of
security filled my heart, and the same gladness might
have been seen to overspread the faces of the other
onlookers. But this joy was of short duration. A
terrible voice was suddenly heard, and we saw
Davesne's father approaching. Almost simultane-
ously my own father came out from the factory, and
a man with a frank, open face and a very black
beard appeared at the door of the cottage from
which the boy had come.

"'You young blackguard,' shouted Davesne,
'you've done this by foul play.'

"'That's not true!' cried my father.

"'What! you again!' exclaimed the brute.

"Then we heard a deep voice with just the least
tremor in it:

" 'My son was never guilty of foul play—and yours is a coward.'

" 'Hallo! . . . It's the stranger . . . Some more fun!'

"The man from the cottage shrugged his shoulders, while Davesne approached with deliberate step and a ferocious expression.

" 'You want a taste of what the others have got?'

"It seemed only too probable he would get it. The carpenter was certainly a strapping fellow and strong as a horse, but Davesne was a veritable fighting beast—the human animal admirably proportioned for the stress and swiftness of attack. The victory of the young son was a welcome surprise to all; but there was no hope of such luck in the case of the father. Meanwhile, my own father had come forward into the meadow, and the villagers looked on at a safe distance, afraid to express their feelings, cunningly neutral, and entirely under the subjection of the tyrant.

" 'What do you want?' said the carpenter. 'What reason have you for attacking me?'

"Although he spoke in a resolute tone he seemed to show some vacillation, and my father made a sign to him to return to his house. It was too late. Davesne had leapt at his throat. There were two or three moments of horrible suspense; then we saw that the carpenter had got clear, and was holding himself on the defensive. Davesne renewed his attack, and delivered many blows, which were parried, or, at any rate, lost most of their force. The carpenter took the offensive in his turn. Davesne had only just time to dodge aside. Then they came up face to face, and it was evident that the brute had met his match. Realizing this, his features hardened and a murderous look came into his eyes. My father, ready to die rather than desert his new ally, was about to take his place at his side.

" 'Stay where you are,' said the other in so stern a voice that my father did not persist. He attacked again, and this time caught Davesne full on the face. The other replied with a shower of blows, one of which got home and made the carpenter stagger. I thought it was all up with him and groaned. But I was wild with delight when I saw him come on again, break Davesne's guard, and with three smashing blows on the jaw, stretch the brute on the ground with blood on his face.

"Then my father and I looked at each other; and no miracle of the spiritual kind, none of the apparitions of heaven-sent beings that used to elevate the souls of men, can ever have caused more exaltation than the ecstasy of joy that blanched our faces. I wanted to go on my knees to the carpenter and his son, who from that moment became for me the highest personification of manhood.

"But the battle was not yet over. Our new-born Hope was not free from doubt. The carpenter had let Davesne get up. The brute had evidently made up his mind for a struggle in which body joins body —for the grip in which main force alone counts. It was obviously the plan best suited to his immense strength now that all his other tactics had failed. He stood for some moments taking stock of his opponent, his eyes bloodshot, his mouth set in a

revolting intensity of hatred. The carpenter himself seemed a little daunted as he watched every
movement of Davesne. At last came the rush.
There was a confused intermingling of limbs and
bodies; then the antagonists became locked together,
their positions being about equally favorable. With
a last supreme effort, Davesne lifted the other off
his legs; we thought this was the end. And so
indeed it was, but in another sense. The carpenter
fell on his feet, and with lightning swiftness took on
the offensive. Davesne doubled and twisted in his
grip, but borne down in that close embrace, he found
himself touching the earth with his shoulders.

"'Do you give in?' said the carpenter.

"Davesne made a desperate struggle to rise; the
carpenter forced him back and pinned him to the
ground.

" 'Do you give in?'

"Then a hoarse voice muttered:

" 'I give in.'

"They both rose. Davesne stood irresolute for
one moment; but finally he accepted his defeat, and
moved away with bowed head.

"My father rushed up to the carpenter in a trans-
port of joy, and I murmured words of heartfelt
gratitude to my youthful deliverer. Pressing round
us, the peasants raised loud cheers for the victor.

"Such is the most notable passage of my life,
which I cannot even now recall without a thrill of
emotion; such is also the origin of the closest of my
attachments. My father became the carpenter's
close friend, and the son became mine. This double
alliance resulted in much happiness, for later on our

two fathers, as the result of some fortunate circumstances, became partners in a successful scheme for clearing land. As for me, I found in Charles an inseparable companion and a loyal protector, gentle as he was brave. My devotion to him became almost a religion, and even now the happiest days of my life are those we spend together either here in Paris or in his forest-surrounded home in the country."

ROBERT SCHEFFER

XXVII

THE MOTHER

By Robert Scheffer

HOW and when Jacques and I became friends
matters very little. I think he takes pleasure
in my society because it is natural to me to speak
my mind without reticence or reserve. He, on the
other hand, talks about what he has observed—he
is a great traveler—but as regards himself he main-
tains an obstinate silence. In this way we are human
complements. On the outbreak of war we lost sight
of each other; all I knew of him was that his thorough knowledge of German had enabled him to
offer his services as an interpreter. Towards the
end of last year we met again, and his work keeping
him since that time in Paris, we renewed, so far as
his duties permitted, our old companionship. There
was little change in either of us, and the accounts
he gave of his experiences were immensely interest-
ing to one who had vegetated while so much was
doing, and could contribute nothing to the war but
idle speculations. I remarked, however, the imprint
of suffering in the lines of his face, which I thought
was not to be wondered at considering the nature of
his work. But it appeared there was a more intimate and secret cause for it.

Yesterday afternoon he came to me in a nervous,

agitated state, altogether unlike himself. Before I could ask any questions, he broke out, pacing the floor with long strides:

"I must speak. I must tell my trouble to some one. It has been making me miserable all through the war, and to-day I feel as if my heart is breaking."

I was completely taken aback. He saw it, and went on more calmly:

"Oh! I've not committed any crime. It's sorrow, and sorrow of a most intimate kind. Let me tell you about it; perhaps that will ease my mind. You know nothing, or next to nothing, of my family, except that my father was a worthy man, a wine-merchant, and that he left me my small income. But my mother—well, though her name was French, my mother was a German.

"My mother had never been able to adapt herself to French ways and manners, and at Paris hankered incessantly after the Baden district where she was born. How the marriage came about I do not exactly know; it was a case of love on my father's side, I believe, but more especially one of mutual interests affecting the two families.

"I was an only child, and my parents were devoted to me. My father, who considered me gifted beyond my years, imagined a brilliant career for me; I was to study law, was to be a barrister, Member of Parliament, a Minister. My mother shook her head; she would have liked me to be a poet, a musician, and though she did not put it into words, she believed that I should find Germany the country most suited to my talents and character.

"How can I describe my mother. Dreamy and

sentimental, she passed part of every day at the piano, absorbed in Mendelssohn or Schumann; she loved to interpret Wagner to me, and growing exalted as she played, a dreamy mysticism used to fill her eyes as she said: 'Listen intently: it is the soul of my country overflowing and shedding its blessing on you.' I loved that music, and as I listened, my mother's charming face, beautified by her exaltation, symbolized for me the country of her birth. I did not care so much for the poetry she used to read me—Uhland, Geibel, or Schiller, whom she considered incomparable. I did not understand them; and when she tried to make me like the patriotic poems of Arndt or Koerner, my whole soul rebelled. Some instinctive revolt made me remember that my father was French, and I told her so. Then she would stroke my hair and say sadly: 'Poor child, you ought to have had a different father.'

"My father knew nothing of all this; he fully believed that in spite of her German ways, his wife was quite content with her adopted country, and he never troubled himself about my double heredity and its possible influence. And no harm might have come from it had he lived, but he died before I had grown out of boyhood, and the course of my existence was entirely changed.

"My mother went back to live with her family, and under the pretext that it would be useful for me to know German thoroughly, I was sent to a boarding-school at Heilbronn, Wurtemburg. I was not happy there—not that they ill-treated me, but they were completely tactless, making me feel their, not hostility towards the French, but a kind of sympathetic pity. For example, one day when a professor had been extolling the virtues and greatness of Germany, he said to me: 'You have a share in all this. You are half-German, and the day will come when you will *have* to be wholly German.' And he went on to describe the dream of Germany ruling the world and regenerating mankind under the inspiring genius of the Emperor. I protested hotly; but he only burst into a fit of laughter in which my schoolfellows joined.

"I spent my holidays alternately with relatives of my father or with my mother. My mother . . . I hardly recognized her, she had so completely changed. She had bloomed into a different kind of being. Dreamy and wistful in bygone days, she was now expansive and full of merriment. She laughed heartily at the broadest German jokes. The keyboard of the piano was no longer touched with dreamy restraint; its notes thundered. Her voice vibrated as she sang passionate 'lieder.' She dressed richly and with a bad taste that shocked me. She had become an excessive eater. I could not bear to see her enjoying an atmosphere of pretentious vulgarity. She would kiss me, saying: 'Well, you're happy here, Jacques, aren't you? You feel that you're lucky to be growing up among a race of wonderful people, don't you?' And she would run on interminably in the same strain, repeating that she was happy, and taking no notice of my uneasiness. Her brother—my uncle—noticed it for her. 'Oh, the little Frenchie!' he scoffed, 'he is prejudiced against us now, but the day will come when he will *have* to love us!' I thought of my father and all he had told me of the agonies of 1870, and my eyes filled with tears.

"Happy, yes, my mother was happy, more than happy, and in a way I little imagined. One evening —it was during the Easter holidays—she beckoned me to her side. An air of great festivity permeated the house, which I put down to preparations for Easter. But I was wrong. Without any leading up to it, she said: 'Jacques, I am going to be married.' I stared at her, stupefied. She laughed. 'You think I'm too old for that?' No, my mother was still quite young, younger than I had ever known her, exuberant to an overwhelming degree. My throat contracted with a kind of anguish. 'And who is it?' I murmured. 'Dr. Weber.' Dr. Weber, red-faced, fat, gold-spectacled, vain, prosy . . . 'A German,' I cried. 'Naturally,' she replied. A heart-twist sent burning tears to my eyes . . . She looked at me with cold displeasure, reproaching me for being too sensitive and shutting my eyes to the realities of life. But later on she kissed me, assuring me that the marriage would make no change in our relationship; then she praised the attainments and character of my future stepfather, and finally I was dismissed with the information that she had made all arrangements for completing my education, and that I was free to choose my path in life—in Germany or in France.

"I could not bear the idea of meeting Dr. Weber again, and next day I took refuge with some relations of my father.

"For a long time I reproached myself bitterly for having acted like this towards my mother. It was about 1895, and there was at that period no hatred of Germany, rather an instinctive antipathy not unmingled with admiration. But it was no use reasoning with myself; I felt a kind of shame about this second marriage; it seemed to me that in some subtle way the humiliation involved me, and that sensation was strong enough to make me recoil from companionship in directions where my parentage was known.

"From that time onwards I knew nothing of my mother but what her letters told me. Yet I loved her, and loved her with all the more ardor because I needed her and she was so far away. I read her letters eagerly, trying to discover in them some token of affection and tenderness. If there had been one word of real love, I would have asked forgiveness, and would have approached her husband in a friendly spirit. But they were frigid, with a forbidding note of pendantry in their eternal good advice, and when she told me she had given birth to a son, Eric, I knew the separation was definite, and that for her I had become a foreigner.

"Study and travel in different countries kept me from dwelling on my curious orphanhood, and I grew to look on it with a calmness that verged on indifference. Or I thought I did. But indifference is apparently only a passing sleep of the feelings, for I have just had an experience that has awakened emotions which prove that, though I have not heard from her since the outbreak of war, nothing can alter my love for her.

"You know that a few days ago a Zeppelin was brought down near Paris. The pilot, dangerously wounded, was taken prisoner. I have not seen him, but his papers were sent to me for translation. There were letters addressed to 'Lieutenant Eric Weber' and—they were in my mother's handwriting!

"I cannot describe the agony with which I read those letters, the misery of having to translate them for others. And my suffering was not caused by the fact that my brother, my half-brother, had come over to try to murder our civilians; it was as the son of my mother that I suffered. For all the letters began 'My only son; My dear and only son . . .' Apparently I have ceased to exist for her.

"Has she forgotten me? Has she abjured me? My mother is alive, and yet I have no mother. Can you realize what that means, you who have a mother, a real French mother, who loves you dearly?"

MARCELLE TINAYRE

XXVIII

THE HOME-COMING

By Marcelle Tinayre

THE young widow looked at the small gray house
that seemed to stand waiting for her at the end
of the garden, and the path that led to it appeared
much longer and narrower than it used to be, to such
an extent had the weeds spread over the gravel
where nobody now walked. The pear-trees were in
full leaf; the branches of the lime-trees, which had
not been cut back for the last two years, were waving over the crumbling top of the wall. The nettles,
now in flower, were everywhere, choking the rose-
bushes which had run wild. And in spite of the sun
and the song of the birds, you felt cold in this garden, and spoke with a lowered voice as if you were
in a cemetery.

An old servant, who had received the traveler
and was carrying her dressing-bag, was explaining
the bad state of the garden.

"If Madame had only let me know sooner, I would
have had the house in perfect order and weeded
the garden, and everything would have been as it
was before . . . But I've done my best; I have
cleaned the drawing-room and the other rooms without altering anything, and Madame will find even
the smallest thing exactly where it used to be . . ."

The widow nodded her assent. She could not speak. Her clear eyes, young eyes that tears had tortured but had not faded, filled and became fixed on the shadow on the gravel of her long widow's veil which rose from time to time in the breeze, and fell back like a tired wing. On this same gravel, the caprice of the sun and wind had not so long ago fashioned other shadows, but they used to be of white skirts and gay silken scarves; and often a slanting sunbeam had laid at the feet of the young lovers a clear-cut presentment of two silhouettes closely drawn together. . . . How far away it all seemed now! Those perfect evenings, love, happiness, peace—they had vanished like the shadows. One August morning the happy master of the little gray house, the happy husband of this young woman with luminous eyes, had gone forth, a soldier among many soldiers. . . . He was not to return, and for two years his widow had kept away from the home that was so full of tender memories . . .

But at last, with a cruel tightening of the heartstrings, she had resolved to go back, and she did so unable to decide whether she was making a pilgrimage or committing a sacrilege. She would have liked the hall-door to have remained for ever closed, enshrining all those souvenirs of him and of her, shutting in all the warmth and vitality of the love the house had witnessed and contained. This mourning woman had found a strange pleasure in thinking of the rooms, the furniture, the ornaments, as dumb and cherished creatures—sentient creatures, who remembered the beloved master and were waiting happily, with faithful patience, for his return, *because they did not know that he was dead.*

She had not told any one of this quaint and tender fancy, born in a passionate soul where grief had for two years fostered and strengthened ideas full of mysticism and touching superstition. Her friends did not understand her apparent neglect of the gray house and the old garden, or why, for the first year of her widowhood, she went far away to a village in the mountains. And some women, always ready to pronounce severe verdicts, had declared that Juliette was lacking in devotion to her husband's memory. But Juliette did not wish to pose as a modern Artemisia. She did not flaunt the emphatic and solemn widowhood that is always reminiscent of the day of the funeral. Her black dress passed unnoticed in the crowd. Her black veil was as modest as her face. She did not make a parade of posthumous faithfulness which might have been a tacit rebuke to other widows who, perhaps not strong enough to stand alone, had consoled themselves too quickly . . .

The servant went in first, and from the inside pushed back the persiennes of the drawing-room windows. On the threshold Juliette hesitated. When at last with slow steps she entered the hall, its coolness sent a chill through her. Once again she saw the English engravings on the walls, the antlers, the trophy of arms on the large panel, and the green cane furniture with yellow cushions. These things exhaled a perfume of the past which intoxicated her as would a sweet and fatal philtre. She did not stop. Slowly, with the strange automatism one feels in dreams, she crossed the drawing-room with its Persian hangings, where the piano was still open, where two armchairs were drawn close together near a little table still covered with old magazines and newspapers. And still with the same measured steps, she went towards the corner-room that caught the first rays of the morning sun, the windows wreathed by clusters of roses, the room that had been their resting-place, their nest, the center of their world.

Bottles and silver brushes shone on the dressing-table. A mauve dressing-gown had been thrown across an armchair. In a crystal bowl there was still the end of a cigarette that had not burnt out, and a pair of gold sleeve-links that had been thrown there in the hurry of departure. And the railway time-table for July, 1914, was lying on the floor, crumpled up . . .

Juliette looked at the silken counterpane, and her thoughts went to the slightly-hollowed place into which she used to complain she always slipped when she fell asleep against the big strong body that was truly the flesh of her flesh, the complement of herself in the living substance of another being.

Nothing was changed. The room, the furniture, the light, the branches of the rose-tree against the window pane—and the bed . . .

The house of happiness knew of nothing but its happiness. It was calm and confident. No one, not even the nettles in the garden or the spiders in the dark corners, had told it the terrible news.

But Juliette felt that if she recognized all these things, they did not recognize her . . The brightly-hued chintz, the dainty furniture, the little familiar objects, did not welcome her; they were hostile to this sad stranger dressed in black.

A flood of tears gushed up from her heart and filled her eyes—burning tears that seemed to flow from the source of her being, and carry away with them some essential part of her inner life. She fell upon the bed, clutching at the counterpane and the pillow, pressing her mouth into the pale satin. And between her sobs she gasped:

"He is dead! . . . He is dead! He will never came back again! . . . He is dead! . . ."

Then, her strength all spent, she lay still with outstretched arms in a silence that was more tragic than her weeping, while slowly and mysteriously all round her the soul of the house went into mourning.

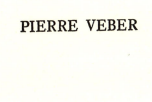

PIERRE VEBER

XXIX

WIDOW FOIGNEY

By PIERRE VEBER

MY old friend, the learned Professor Lucien Berthe, said to me: "You have just passed your last examination, and you are now a fully-fledged doctor. You're fairly good-looking, you dress well, you talk very little, you look trustworthy, and have an air of listening to what is said to you even when you are thinking of something else. With these points in your favor, you are sure to get a nice little practice together; after that, invent a remedy and you will make a lot of money, and if you end by discovering a new malady, there will be a fortune for you. At the beginning, choose a thickly-populated neighborhood where there are a lot of lower middle-class people; they make the best patients because they lead sedentary lives, and are frequently ailing. Take a flat on the ground-floor in some house where there is no other doctor—it will be hard to find, but it does exist."

"And ought I to furnish this flat?"

"Certainly. Didn't your uncle, President Blom, leave you some money the other day? How much was it?"

"Ten thousand francs."

"It's very little . . . but you must make it do. You must furnish a waiting-room, a consulting-room, a dining, and a bed-room. You can get the things second-hand. Look at the fourth page of the newspapers."

I followed the advice of my old chief. Among the advertisements I picked out one that read: *Complete household effects, elegant, good as new, for sale owing to death. Apply to Madame V. F., 224 rue Saint-Marc.* I went to this address and asked the concierge if Madame V. F. lived there.

"Ah! Madame the Widow Foigney? The second floor to the left."

I went upstairs and rang the bell. An old man-servant dressed in black took me into a charming little drawing-room. I told him the object of my visit, and he bowed and went away. Left thus alone, I discreetly examined the armchairs, passed a knowing hand over the desk, the center-table, the card-table, fingered the curtains; everything seemed in capital condition; and certainly Madame the Widow Foigney was a very excellent housewife, for everything was exquisitely clean. The door opened, and in came a pretty woman, very fair, inclined to be plump, with an amusing little face and a piquant nose. She was dressed in deep mourning, but her face showed no traces of grief. She asked me to sit down.

"Monsieur," she said, "let me begin by telling you that you can have these things very cheap. . . . I am obliged to go to Antwerp. My people live there, and as the death of my poor husband necessitates my leaving Paris, I am going to stay for a

time with my mother.   Except for my servant, Noel,
I am quite alone here."

"The old servant who opened the door?"

"Yes, such a devoted creature.   My husband died
in his arms."

Here Madame Foigney's eyes filled with tears.
I hastened to express my regret for having inadver-
tently suggested such sad thoughts.

"Oh, no, Monsieur!   It is I who am silly not to
succeed in banishing them.   But I was so happy
during the six months I had my dear husband with
me."

"Only six months?"

"Yes, just six months of happiness.   You will see
that the furniture is practically new.   The more so
that we had· been married four months before we
bought it.   We spent the first few months, our honey-
moon, at Antwerp with my mother.   Ah!   Those
four months!   If you only knew, Monsieur . . . if
you only knew. . . . And then just after we came
here my poor husband fell ill."

"What was the matter with him?" I asked a little
uneasily.

"Oh, nothing contagious.   My husband had heart-
disease, and he was removed at once to a nursing
home.   The furniture and bedding are intact."

"So much the better."

Madame the Widow Foigney did not seem to
have heard my involuntary exclamation.   She was
talking again of her dear lost one, of the wonderful
qualities he possessed, of the devotion of the elderly
Noel—ah! those old family servants!   I was beginning to see that she was a woman with a very

warm heart and fine feelings, and I found myself thinking with some envy of this Foigney, who had been lucky enough to be loved by such a charming person. The minutes flew by without my making any allusion to the furniture, and it was Madame Foigney who returned to the subject.

"But I must be boring you, Monsieur, telling you all those things that have no interest for any one but me. Would you like to see the furniture? I have decided to sell everything, from the chandeliers to the saucepans. I don't want to keep a single thing that will recall my lost happiness."

After we had examined everything in the drawing-room, she took me to the Henri II dining-room; it is curious to find how frequently this eclipsed monarch presides at the repasts of the French middle-classes, while Louis XV alternates with Louis XVI in superintending conversation in the drawing-rooms where people talk too much.

But Madame de Pompadour had organized the elegant discretion of the bedroom, where twin beds stood close together under one canopy. I remarked that one bed would be enough for me, that I was not married.

"Bah!" replied Madame Foigney. "You will marry before long. No one can live alone."

I do not know why this phrase had a great effect on me.

When we returned to the drawing-room I asked the price of the things.

"Really I hardly know what to say . . . I don't understand these matters. What ought I to ask? . . . let me think. We bought everything at the best house-furnishers in Paris—Servaings. It all cost twenty-five thousand francs. I can show you the bills . . ."

"That's surely very dear . . ."

"I should not ask you to pay the full sum . . . though everything is new, it is still what one calls 'second-hand furniture.' Suppose I let you have it for . . . let me see . . . twenty thousand francs?"

This was double the amount I had meant to spend. Madame Foigney understood my hesitation.

"Well, then, suppose we say fifteen thousand and be done with it? . . . If it is not convenient to pay all at once, you can give me two-thirds now, and the balance in six months' time."

I would have accepted at once, and with gratitude, but I felt I ought to seem to be considering the offer. As a matter of fact, the charm and grace of the seller had made an immense impression on me, and I did not like the idea of not seeing her again. I told her I would give a definite answer in two days' time. She did not try to hide her disappointment.

"It's not very convenient to wait like that," she said. "I wanted to get away by the end of the week."

"So soon?" I exclaimed involuntarily.

Madame Foigney blushed; yes, she blushed. . . . But she was not displeased; my sincerity was too evident, and all she said was: "Very well, I shall expect you on Thursday." The elderly Noel opened the door ceremoniously for me, and I found myself looking with friendliness at this fine old servant, whom I should have been glad to purchase with the furniture.

As I went home, I called to see the Professor Lucien Berthe, to whom I related the incidents of the afternoon. He gave me a word of warning.

"Take care what you're doing. . . . I believe your pretty widow is making a fool of you . . . Fifteen thousand silver francs! And you call that a bargain?"

I almost lost my temper, and I began to wonder seriously whether my good old chief was not threatened with senile decay.

I was also impelled to take all my friends into my confidence about my visit to 224, rue Saint Marc. "If she is as pretty as all that, this little Foigney, why don't you try to console her?" Some men are very coarse . . . At length the great day came. It was impossible to sleep on Wednesday night, for a curious idea had come to me. I struggled against it, but it only grew stronger. It was stupid, idiotic . . . so much the worse . . . there it was! . . .

I dressed myself with unusual care before setting out for rue Saint Marc. The old Noel opened the door. He remembered me.

"Ah! It is the gentleman who called on Tuesday. I will go and tell Madame."

Madame Foigney herself came to take me to the drawing-room. She was even prettier than when I saw her before—or I was intoxicated with love at first sight. I felt that I was on the point of committing an irreparable mistake. Meanwhile Madame Foigney was talking.

"I have been waiting impatiently for you. Two or three people have come since you were here, and have offered me more than the sum we agreed on.

. . . But I was bound by my promise, and I told them I could not give a reply till to-morrow . . . I have also had a visit from a gentleman who imagined extraordinary things . . . that I, too, was for sale, and who took upon himself to . . ."

"The beast!" I cried hotly. "I'd have settled him quickly if I'd been here."

"You are very kind, but I rang the bell, and Noel came and soon showed him out."

"But it's horrible! To think that you should be at the mercy of any cad who likes to force himself in like that! . . . You, so delicate, so exquisite, to think of you being exposed defenseless to such insults!"

I was off! Carried clean away by the lyricism of heroic amorousness, I let myself go.

It was in vain that Madame Foigney tried to stop my torrent of passionate commonplaces . . . I talked and I talked. But even as I poured it out, the observer that every man has in him was listening with a surprised: "What's the matter? What's all this about?" But it was no use. I went right on to the end: I told Madame Foigney that I wanted to marry—and to marry her! "No one can live alone"—had she not said it herself? Her sadness would wear off as time went by, and I would do my best to help her to regain her interest in life. I was a doctor, backed up by the heads of the profession: I would work day and night to make a position; with her to help me, nothing would be impossible. I had fallen in love with her at first sight. Her sad little story had gone to my heart, and I had sworn that I would help her back to happiness. She should forget the past, leave it all behind her—all except her dear old Noel . . .

It was some minutes before I stopped. Madame Foigney was listening with her face buried in her handkerchief, her body convulsed by sobs.

"You are crying! . . . Oh, don't cry. . . . I beg you not to cry. . . ."

But no! She was not crying. She was laughing . . . shaking with laughter.

"How funny!" she cried. "Oh, how very funny!"

It makes me angry to see a widow laugh, and I was the more so because I felt I looked like an imbecile. It was some little time before she was able to explain.

"No, dear Monsieur, I will not be your wife."

"And why? . . . Aren't you a widow?"

"I am a wife, and my husband is very much alive. He is Noel, the old servant. He is really Servaing, the upholsterer. As business was not at all good, we invented this widow-trick to sell 'complete household effects.' It has been a great success. Since you were here, we've sold all this three times over. We just bring the things in and take them out again. . . . In a year we shall have enough to retire from business. . . . Don't you think I do the widow very well? . . . Even my husband begins to believe in it sometimes, and sheds tears over his own death. . . ."

"He is not at all bad in his part either, looks the old servant to the life," I said with some bitterness.

"Come, come, don't be angry. . . . Remember, it is very nice of me to have taken you into my confidence.   Don't stand on your dignity. . . . I'll let you have everything for twelve thousand."

I hesitated, and she added in a low voice: "Say 'yes,' and as soon as the things are in your flat, I will go and help you to arrange them."

I said yes, and she kept her word.   But I must confess that both the furniture and the acquaintance came to pieces very quickly—shoddy stuff!